The
Right
STUD

WALL STREET JOURNAL BESTSELLING AUTHOR
ILSA MADDEN-MILLS
USA TODAY BESTSELLING AUTHOR
TIA LOUISE

This book is a work of fiction. Names, characters, places, and incidents are products of the author's imagination or are used fictitiously. Any resemblance to actual events or locales or persons, living or dead, is entirely coincidental.

The Right Stud
Copyright © Ilsa-Louise Books, 2018
All rights reserved.

Cover design by Shanoff Formats
Photography by Wander Aguiar

To our our amazing readers, girl-power believers, goat enthusiasts, and lovers of sexy abs everywhere.

The Right **STUD**

By Ilsa Madden-Mills & Tia Louise

Wall Street Journal *bestselling author Ilsa Madden-Mills and* USA Today *bestselling author Tia Louise are back with an all-new romantic comedy filled with Southern sass and steamy scenes that will have you laughing out loud and fanning yourself. Pour the sweet tea and get ready…*

"The best way to get over your sh**ty ex-fiancé is to get under a shiny new stud…"

As soon as Mr. Tall, Blond, and Handsome walks into that bar, I know he's the hook-up I need to get over stupid Cheater Kyle.

A few stolen kisses in a dark hallway, and I'm pretty sure we're headed for a home run—until he disappears without a trace.

Whatever. Men are all snakes in the grass, and I don't need a new one anyway.

I resolve to forget about his perfect lips (and chest of steel) and instead focus on turning my Granny's old beach house into a profitable B&B.

What I don't expect is for him to show up the next day *in my kitchen*!

You see, my sexy mystery man is none other than Jax Roland, the drop-dead gorgeous home improvement star of *The Right Stud,* and he's got an offer I can't refuse.

With a suitcase in one hand and a hammer in the other, he wants to move in and renovate my old house while he films his new show.

But my roommate has secrets, and they threaten to rip our blossoming friendship—and possible love—apart.

When push comes to shove, is Jax really *The Right Stud* or is he just another nail in the coffin of love?

Chapter 1

Ashton

My ankle turns, and the heel on my left stiletto breaks off right before I open the door to the bar. *Dammit.* I clench my hands and want to throw it across the road, but at this point, I'm determined to suck it up and go inside anyway.

I've been through three wardrobe changes and waited through four traffic lights to get to the Smoky Siren, the newest (and only) late-night bar in Palmetto, South Carolina, and nothing is going to stop me now. *Right, Starship?*

Hobbling over to a black wrought-iron bench beside a lamppost adorned with hanging baskets of petunias, I take a seat and peer through the large, front window. I'll give it to the owners, they've done a great job creating a funky, aquatic vibe with turquoise blue accents and iridescent fixtures. It's packed to the gills on a Saturday night, and couples spill out the doors laughing and talking.

They're mostly tourists and beach vacationers, but according to my friend Lulu, it's *The Place* to find a fast fling. She'd know, since she knows everything going on in our tiny clutch of communities along the coast.

My eyes go to my busted shoe and my bravado deflates. *What am I doing here?* I should be home on the couch in my flannel pajamas eating Ben and Jerry's Wedding Cake Wonder and watching *Fixer Uppers.*

I inhale sadly. I'm not supposed to be alone tonight. I'm supposed to be ensconced in wedded bliss, celebrating my six-month anniversary as Mrs. Dr. Kyle Nelson.

That's right.

Six months, three hours ago, I should have been showing up at the Charleston First United Methodist Church in a beaded, mermaid-tail wedding gown that cost more than five thousand dollars, which I'd ended up reselling on eBay for less than half.

Note to self: bridal boutiques do not take back dresses nor do catering establishments refund your ten-thousand-dollar deposit.

I cringe before catching sight of my reflection in the glass. At least being cheated on has done wonders for my figure. I'm down ten pounds since the break-up and can even fit into this dress from five years ago. Red and silky with a deep plunging V-neck, it clings to my curves. I may not have love, but at least my body is on point.

"Excuse us!" A young couple holding hands brushes past the bench a little too close as they rush to the double doors and slip inside the bar.

They're too busy gazing into each other's eyes to look up, and I think of everything I've lost. Scorned-woman rage washes over me, and I want to scream *LOVE SUCKS!* at them.

See? Hooking up with someone tonight is a terrible idea. Anyway, Mrs. Capshaw, my one guest at the B&B I own and operate (and love), is probably still awake. She might be up for a *Gilmore Girls* marathon.

We love that show. She even calls me Lorelai sometimes, which I take as a high compliment. Who needs men when I have my own bed and breakfast on the beach? I need a cat—but just one, since more than one means I'm on my way to being a crazy cat lady.

Taking off both shoes, I stand and spin around to head back to my car just as my phone rings. My breath catches, my chest squeezes, and part of me—the stupid, sad part—hopes it's Kyle calling to let me know, after all this time, he's finally seen the truth. He made a horrible mistake when he cheated.

It isn't Kyle, which is fine, because I wouldn't take that bastard back no matter how hard he begged.

It's only Lulu.

I exhale and tap the green circle. "Wasn't it enough that you were just at my house and picked out my entire outfit?"

"Are you there yet?" My best friend since kindergarten asks. "Or are you standing at the front door talking yourself out of going in?"

With the phone to my ears, I lift my chin and gaze at the starry night sky. "I'll have you know I'm at the bar, and I just ordered a martini."

"You're a sucky liar. Always have been. Remember that time you told me I had a booger on my cheek so I'd run to the bathroom and *you'd* get to kiss Reggie Wallace at Shelia's sweet sixteen?"

"Oh my God, how do you remember these things?" I cry. "And for your information, he can't French kiss worth a lick. Anyway, how do you know I'm lying? It's very rude to accuse people of—"

Her gum smacks as she chews. "I'm parked on the street watching you, scaredy-pants. Why are you holding your shoes?"

"What?" My head jerks around and sure enough, I spot her curly red head sitting inside her Prius.

She waves at me enthusiastically. "Followed you."

"Don't you have five dogs and a goat to babysit?"

"Jean Claude is a ram, and I'm not here to party with you. I'm here to make sure you walk in that door and have a drink, preferably with a hot man. You haven't left your house in a six months."

"Not true..." It's a mumbled reply, because she's right.

In the beginning it had been hard to leave the house because every time I'd go outside I'd bump into someone giving me a pitying look and asking how I was doing.

Now I feel like they're looking at me like it's time to stop wallowing. Seriously?

Betrayal flashes in my chest anew as I remember catching Kyle cheating on me with his dental hygienist, Monica with the good veneers. She'd been using that mouth to go down on—*No! I will not replay the sight again.*

Lulu cuts through my cringe-fest down memory lane. "The best way to get over an old, shitty guy is to get under a new, shiny one. Now get in there! It's time."

I roll my eyes even though she can't see them.

"And don't roll your eyes at me!"

I groan. "Fine, but I think going home is a better idea." I search for excuses. "My heel just broke off, plus I have Mrs. C to consider. She'll expect me to put out muffins in the morning."

"Well, I expect you to put out muffins tonight!"

"I don't even know what that means—"

"It means break off your other heel and get your butt in the Smoky Siren! Mrs. C and her foul-mouthed parrot will be there when you get home."

I heave out a long sigh. Lulu's right about one thing: I have been spending a lot of time in overalls, doing my best to repair my grandmother's sprawling, hundred-year-old home by the sea.

I thought I was doing it for Kyle and me, and eventually our four beautiful children... Until it all went up in smoke. Or laughing gas, I suppose.

Squeezing the phone against my shoulder, I turn my good shoe over and twist off the heel then put it back on my foot. It's a weird feeling walking in heelless stilettos, but I know if I go all the way home for new ones, I won't come back. Plus I really don't care what my shoes look like. Straightening my shoulders, I walk with purpose toward the door.

Lulu laughs. "That's my girl."

"I'm hanging up now," I grumble.

"Call me when you get home. I want to hear all about it."

"Walk all those dogs over in the morning for breakfast. Leave the goat at home."

"Deal."

—

"I don't have all night." The enormous bartender's dark brow lowers, and he stares at me expectantly.

My mind blanks, and I try to think of what I want. I always panic when bartenders put me on the spot like this. I want to be sophisticated and order something like a martini, no ice, two olives. Instead I usually just ask for a glass of wine.

Not tonight!

"I'll have a margarita." My voice wobbles, and I clear my throat. "A margarita!" I say louder, with confidence.

I might be standing on two broken heels, but it's a stand for jilted women everywhere. I'm better than Monica with the good veneers, and Kyle should've seen it. It's his loss.

The bulky bartender's expression is bored as he quickly

upends a plastic bottle of lime-green margarita mix while simultaneously pouring Jose Cuervo into an ice-filled silver shaker. Three loud rattles later, and he's dumping it all into a large, salt-rimmed glass and passing it to me. I coolly hand him a ten and wait for my change, then slip him a dollar tip.

Turning my back to the bar, I look around the packed establishment. What the heck do I do now? "Despacito" blasts overhead, and a few women let out shrieks as they race to the dance floor. I stay put, tapping my broken-heeled foot and sipping my drink. I just need a little more liquid courage before I take on the male clientele. Also, I don't know if I can seriously work my mojo to Justin Bieber. I need more Rolling Stones... "Brown Sugar" or "Honkey Tonk Woman." It's possible my margarita is kicking in.

I frown into my already half-empty glass trying to remember the last time I had hard liquor.

"You live around here?" I gasp and almost toss my drink at the male voice shouting over my shoulder.

Blinking quickly, I look around, hoping for the best, and... instant disappointment. Standing beside me is a nice-enough looking guy. His light brown hair is combed neatly in a side part and brown, oversized glasses are perched on his nose. He has a mustache. He waggles his eyebrows.

Coughing, I shake my head. "I'm sorry. What?"

"I said do you live around here?"

"Uh..." Do I want him to know where I live? "Sort of."

"That's a funny thing to say. Sort of? Sort of what?"

Jesus, take the wheel. "I mean, my family lives here. I'm just visiting... from Manitoba."

"Manitoba!" His eyebrows shoot up, and he steps closer, still speaking too loudly. "That's in Canada, right? I've always wanted to go to Canada. Imagine what everybody would say if I told them I had a girlfriend in Canada." He actually snorts. "What's your favorite part about living in Canada?"

Shit! I don't know anything about living in Canada. I thought it would get rid of him, thinking I live so far away. "Uh…" I look all around the bar, racking my brains. "The… uh… syrup?"

His chin rises, and he nods slowly, knowingly. "Maple trees."

"Oh, well." I put my empty margarita glass on the bar. "I'd better go… now."

"Roger." He sticks a hand toward me.

"Sorry?" Is he agreeing with me?

"Name's Roger, and you are?"

Oh.

"Ashton." I can only keep up with so many lies. "Like I said, I've got to go now."

"I'll walk you out—"

"To the bathroom!" I hastily add.

He takes a step back when I add that part. *Thank the maples.* "I'll just be waiting right here." He turns his handshake into a pat on my arm. "I'll order you another drink!"

"Oh, you don't have to—"

"It's no problem at all! Just a little southern hospitality for our neighbor to the north!"

I'm not the whole freakin' country. "Whatever." I hastily make my way through the thickening crowd away from him, toward the safety of the women's restroom. I'm almost there when I hear him calling after me.

"If it gets too warm, we can always go for a cooling swim!"

In his dreams, but I'm not turning back now. I'll just have to get comfortable in the ladies' room and wait… and hope he gives up before I come out again.

I'm going to kill Lulu.

This was such a bad idea.

Chapter 2

Jax

I'll never let my sister set me up on a blind date again.

Of course the twenty-something across from me appears fine on the surface, and she *is* pretty. But underneath, she's looking for a husband. I knew it the moment she sat across from me at the Smoky Siren, gazing at me with those big eyes.

Exhale.

For starters, I don't do relationships, and I'm definitely not on the market for a wife.

Still, my sister hopes I'll meet some sweet southern girl, leave my condo in Manhattan, and move back to Charleston, where I'll live happily ever after right next door to her and her three kids.

I'm here for a job. What I hope will make a really interesting segment for *The Right Stud*, my Number 1 home improvement show on YouTube. Yep, it's doing really well, but I need something bigger, something my producer can pitch to her friends at HGTV.

And as soon as the week ends, I'm back to the Big Apple and my day job.

"...and then I graduated with honors from Ole Miss and decided to open a bridal shop here in Charleston." My setup flutters long eyelashes at me. "A lot of people tell me I'm ridiculously romantic, but all I say is, well, if you're in the business of love, then you have to be ready for Mr. Right at all times. Don't you agree?" She sips her white wine, pinky finger up.

"Hmm." I take a sip of scotch, swirling the amber liquid around in my glass.

I'm bored out of my mind, but I have to give it to my sister Bernice, she knows how to pick 'em. The girl in question—I can't remember her name—is definitely my type: honey-blonde hair, slim, nice tits.

I'm just not interested.

Now that I'm in my thirties, I prefer to date women who view the world through a similar lens—no attachments, live and let live. Life is too short, and there are far too many fish in the sea to swim alongside only one for the rest of my life.

The door opens, and a curvy brunette in a red dress enters the Siren. She has an unusual walk—wobbly?—and as I watch, she straightens her spine and marches to the bar like a soldier headed into battle.

My eyes follow her for some reason, almost as if I know her. Maybe it's the determined expression on her face or the way she scans the crowd resolutely. She doesn't look like she wants to be here. *Welcome to the party, princess.*

I can't help but notice she's pretty, with hair that falls down her back in shiny waves. I'm not the only one checking her out. From my angle at the table, I see a geeky guy in a brown corduroy jacket giving her an eyebrow waggle. Her reaction to him makes me chuckle softly. She inhales deeply, and the motion causes her chest to rise, bringing my attention to her full breasts pressing against the fabric—

"So what's your favorite color?"

I blink, looking back at Bride Girl. "What? Who cares?"

Hurt flashes over her perfectly made-up face, and I grab the reins. Bernie would kill me for being a dick-hole to this otherwise nice person. I need to get my head in the game. Be a gentleman. Stop fantasizing about running interference for Red Dress —even though every time I glance her way, I see her squirming more in an attempt to get away from Corduroy Boy.

"I just thought it would be a good way to get to know each other." Bride Girl sniffs. "I'm sorry if it's too mundane for you."

I shake my head and reach across the table to pat her hand lightly. "No, I'm sorry for the short answer. The truth is, I'm completely wiped from my flight. I had a shitty week, and I honestly didn't expect to meet someone so creative for dinner."

True story. My sister had sprung this on me. I'd expected to be eating alone tonight so I could prep for my meeting tomorrow about the rehab at the B&B. I'm anxious to meet the owner, "Ms. Hall," who I imagine is an older lady, just by the formality of her tone.

She messaged me online about renovating her house, and it sounds like a dream come true for TV—a hundred year old home smack dab on the South Carolina coastline. Talk about history and setting, plus my handsome face—if that doesn't get HGTV's attention, nothing will.

"Okay," she smiles, seeming to buy it.

I force a smile. "My favorite color is…" I glance at the brunette, who's still being chatted up by Short, Beige, and Dorky. She's so far out of his league—but right in mine.

"Hello?"

I blink, coming back to my date. "What?"

Her pink lips tighten. "Your favorite color?"

"Sorry. Ah, red?"

She shrugs, disappointment on her face. "Mine's lavender. I did the best wedding last year where the bridal bouquet was all purple with hyacinth, lavender, and lilacs…"

She drones on, describing in detail the color and layout of the flowers as I suck down the rest of my drink. I lift a hand and signal for the server who'd taken our order earlier to bring me another, but he doesn't see me. Not surprising, since he's occupied with a large table in the back.

Dammit. I need another drink if I'm going to sit here pretending to care about hyacinth bouquets and lace patterns.

"…the best month to get married is April, of course—it's not just a joke. The weather is perfect here, not too hot and not too cold. Don't you agree?"

"Uh-huh." My eyes are back on the brunette as I chew my ice.

Admittedly, I'm a little fascinated by her and glad I can study her reflection in the mirror behind the bar. She's a stunner with an oval face framed by hair the color of rich amber whiskey. I can't make out her eye color from here, but in a perfect world, they would be something memorable, like hazel or gray, a color that changes with whatever mood she's in. I'm pretty sure our eyes meet in the mirror, and I give her my classic, lady-killer grin.

"Are you listening?" My date is pissed.

Fuck. I give myself a mental shake. Obviously, I've been working too hard these past few months trying to juggle my day job in real estate with my online show. I'm completely off my game. It's the whole reason I came to Charleston. I need a damn vacation, not female drama.

I clear my throat. "Yes."

She follows where my eyes have been and checks out the bar

area. "Why do you keep looking over there?"

My eyes follow, and I see things change suddenly between Red Dress and my competition. She quickly puts her drink on the bar and makes her way through the crowd away from him, toward the back. His expression is defeated, and I feel encouraged. *Yes!*

It gives me an idea.

"Honestly, I need a drink and the server hasn't been back." I tilt my head at her wine glass as I stand. "Yours is empty, too. I'll get us two more, yes? Maybe we can dance when I get back?"

She shrugs, her eyes narrowed. She's not in Mensa, but I'm fairly certain Bride Girl knows I'm lying through my teeth. "If you say so."

Before she can utter another word, I head for the bar, just as the woman in red disappears, with corduroy blazer calling after her. *Step aside, Poindexter, it's time for the master to get to work.*

Depositing our empty glasses on the bar, I veer away, disappearing into the crowd of dancers, following her toward the restrooms. The bodies close in behind us like a sea, and I follow the movement of her skirt, swishing over her slim thighs, bouncing with the movement of her cute, round ass.

She stops suddenly, and I slam into her, my chest to her back.

"I'm so sorry," I say, stepping forward and catching her elbows, stopping her from falling forward. "I didn't expect to bump into you."

She looks up at me, her hazel eyes widening. Red-satin pillow lips part. "No, I'm sorry." Her voice is soft, breathy. "I shouldn't have stopped so fast."

We're in a dim hallway with two doors at the opposite ends, and people brush past us, but I'm unaware of them. I stare down at her, drinking in her pretty face. In my peripheral, I can't stop noticing her breasts rising and falling rapidly.

"I was walking too fast," I say with a small grin. "Have we met before? I feel like I've seen you somewhere."

"I don't think so." She shakes her head. "I would remember…but you do look familiar. Funny, right?"

A pretty shade of pink floods her cheeks as she blushes. Her eyes drop to her shoes. She's flustered, and it's sexy as hell.

"Are you from Charleston?" It's such a mundane question, but it's safer than what I want to know—how many times I'll be able to see her and hopefully fuck her in the week I'm here.

Her eyes fly up to mine. "No," she says, and my chest sinks. "I live outside of Palmetto, on the coast."

My chest rises just as fast. "I'm actually visiting there this week. Maybe we can see each other, get dinner one night?" *Or every night, with you as the main course.*

She smiles, exposing straight, white teeth and a little dot of a dimple beside her mouth. I want to lick it, but her grin wavers, her gaze distracted.

"What?" I pull back, curious.

"You have a… something." Stretching out her hand, she lightly touches my face. "Something on your cheek. Just a bit of fuzz."

It's electric, her finger warm against my skin, and I reach up to clasp her hand in mine. It's soft, and something primitive rises in my gut. I step forward, and she doesn't back away. She's into me. My brain knows it. So does my cock.

"What's your name?" My voice is husky, low.

"Ashton," she whispers.

The crowd has dispersed, everyone in their places for the moment, and it's just her and me in the hallway. At six-two, I tower over her petite frame, but she isn't intimidated by me. There's a heavy look in her eyes as she gazes up, and damn, I feel an urge to kiss her.

My inner cave man is yelling for me to take what's mine, but I push him down. *Don't be a ass, Jax.* Still, it's difficult. Underneath my new hair cut, freshly shaven face, and expensive suit, beats the heart of a Neanderthal who's found the girl he wants.

"I like it." Even my tone sounds possessive. "Ashton."

"Is that so?" Her hand is in mine, and she's not pulling away.

Her other hand is on my chest, and those soft, round breasts are rising and falling even faster, pressing hard against the V of her dress.

"Do you live around here?" Her eyes are on my mouth.

The heat between us is intoxicating. I've heard of lust at first sight, but this is the first time I've felt such insane chemistry. Her fingers curl on my shirt, and she pulls me closer. Her lips are cherry red and dewy, juicy and sweet. I must be drunk because all I can think about is tasting them.

But, I can't kiss her without her permission

The hot whisper of her breath is against my skin, and I'm a heartbeat away from saying chivalry be damned. I have no guarantee I'll ever see her again, and I can't live my life without kissing this woman.

"I grew up around here," I manage to answer, "but I'm just in town for a visit. I want to see you again."

She sways forward in my arms, pressing her soft body against my hard chest. She's like a willow in the breeze, or sea grasses, or waves. *God, I sound stupid.*

My thumb rubs across her bottom lip, and she inhales sharply, her lips parting at the pressure. "You have the most gorgeous lips."

Her tongue darts out and touches my finger, and it's all the invitation I need.

Without thinking, I lean down, and I'm gratified to feel her arching up, stretching her body as her hands pull me closer. In a breath our mouths meet, soft and hot and wet. Her lips are full and sweet, and a little moan escapes from her throat.

Fuck! My erection springs to life, and I know she feels it. She doesn't seem to mind. She moves closer, still swaying in that way that's driving me crazy. Is she the siren this fucking bar is named after, because I'm caught in her spell like one of those sailors. I'd follow her into the ocean to my death just for the promise of sinking into her depths…

Our tongues touch, and my dick gets harder. Her mouth opens wider, and I consume her. We're hungry, devouring. I'm moving her mouth with mine, tongues curling, hands everywhere, touching, pulling clothes, grinding. If she's this good fully clothed…

"EXCUSE ME!" a male voice shouts, and I pull back, ready to throw a punch.

Instead, I rest my forearms on the wall on either side of Ashton, caging her against my chest to let the guy pass on his way to the restroom.

He mutters "Get a room" as he passes, and we're both breathing hard, panting and flushed. I look down, and when our eyes meet, we both smile. She exhales a slight laugh, and wonder hangs in the air. It's crackling and electric, and I know how I plan to relax this week.

It only leaves one thing…

"Will you be here a while?" I don't want to stop kissing her, but I know I have to get back to Bride Girl and do the right thing.

I need to pay for her drinks then get her the hell home. My sister will be happy she set me up with someone nice, and she can check it off her list of things to do while big brother is in town. Then I'll race back up here and toss Ashton over my shoulder and carry out the door like a good caveman—and spend the rest of the night jackhammering...

"I don't know." She blinks those sexy eyes up to me as she smiles. "It's kind of late. I was thinking I might call it a night. Unless I have a better offer?"

She waits, her eyes expectant, and I cannot believe this. Is she giving me an open invitation? How could I be cursed with such shitty timing? Here I am on a duty date for my sister, and the sexiest thing I've seen in the last five times I've visited home is holding the door wide open for me.

"Don't call it too soon. I have to run a quick errand, but I'll be right back."

Can we just stop and acknowledge what I'm doing right now? Why are none of the women who call me a man whore or a jerk or a cocky bastard ever around for moments like this? A beautiful—correction, *gorgeous*, sex kitten—who, by the way, got my rocks hard with only a kiss, is putting out all the come-hither signals, and what do I do?

I do the right thing.

I'm going to go out there and take Bride Girl home and pray to all that is just and fair in the universe that when I get back here, Ashton will still be waiting.

"An errand?" Her slim brow furrows, and I see her confidence falter.

"I'll be back before you know it. Just... hold that thought."

Leaning forward, I pull her pillow lips between mine one last time.

She exhales a little sigh, and her fingers tighten on my shirt. Our eyes meet once more, and I groan deeply at having to leave her this way. Damn, doing the right thing.

"Wait for me, beautiful."

She nods.

Turning on my heel, I dash up the short hall and back out into the sea of bodies, pushing them aside as I go. My hand is in my pocket, and I'm fishing out cash. I don't have time to wait for the credit card back and forth. Looking down, I'm holding two twenties. It has to be enough for a glass of wine and a scotch. We didn't get top shelf anything. It's more than enough.

Bride Girl is bouncing a foot and looking all around the bar when I arrive and catch her arm, helping her off her stool.

"Jax!" She immediately starts to protest. "What's going on? I thought we were going to dance—"

"I'm sorry. I got a call while I was in the bathroom. My mom needs me."

Her brow furrows. "What's wrong?"

I shrug. "She heard a strange noise in the house—probably nothing—but it scared her. She's home alone tonight, so I should pop over and make sure everything's okay." God. I'm rambling and I'm such a damn liar. I haven't spoken to my mom on purpose in years. But that's another story.

"Should I go with you?"

Shit. I hide my panic as I usher her to the front door. "No, I'm fine. Let's get you home."

I can't tell if Bride Girl is buying all this, but I don't have time to worry about it. I can feel the seconds clicking by, and I don't know how much longer before Ashton stops waiting. After that taste in the hall, it won't be enough until I have the whole thing.

I've got to get back here.

Fast.

Chapter 3

Ashton

Random Hot Guy never came back.

I waited and waited, sitting at the bar while I tossed back another margarita. The music blared, and I listened to Roger drone on about the benefits of hydroponic gardening versus building up the soil in a sandy landscape such as we have here on the coast. My heart jumped every time the door opened, and it wasn't until the song "Closing Time" started blasting through the speakers that I finally gave up.

I know who I want to take me home, and I don't even know his name.

Part of me was tempted to ask the bartender if he remembered the hot guy with the broad shoulders in a gray suit, but then I figured it would sound silly, so I didn't. Instead, I sat there and daydreamed about him, picturing his chiseled face and full, sensuous lips that memorized mine in that small hallway. His mouth was rough, demanding as his lips pushed mine apart and *claimed me*.

It was the best kiss of my life.

I turned on all the charm, and even as clumsy as I was, he knew I was giving him an open invitation. If his mouth was that good at kissing, I was hot all over imagining what else it was good at doing.

My bravery was totally out of character, but he put me at ease. I trusted him for some reason. Something about him was so familiar, although for the life of me, I couldn't put my finger on exactly what it was. Maybe it was the curve of his smile or those smoldering blue eyes, the deep resonance of his voice…

Whatever. I shove all that aside. He didn't come back, and that's all there is to say. If he'd *really* wanted me, he would have come back like he said he would. His whole *wait for me* was probably just a ruse to get away without getting an argument.

Roger walks me to my car, and I give his forearm a squeeze before telling him goodnight and climbing into my Volkswagen alone.

Disappointment curls in my stomach as I drive my baby blue Bug down the narrow road, all the way out to The Conch Shell, Granny's big ole house on the beach.

At least when I'm here, I always feel like everything's going to be okay.

"You let him leave?" Lulu shrieks in my ear once I'm home and on the couch in my flannel PJs with a pint of Ben & Jerry's in my hand and the Property Brothers on the flatscreen. I stick another bite of creamy goodness in my mouth and savor the flavor of gooey cookie dough chunks mixed with salted caramel.

"What else could I do? He said he had to run an errand. I couldn't exactly chase after him. Ugh." I cringe remembering how I'd pretty much thrown myself at him in the hallway. "Face it. I attacked him with my lips, and he blew me off."

The line is silent except for a heavy sigh from Lulu, and I figure she's troubleshooting. "What kind of errand would a guy have at ten o'clock on a Friday night?"

"Exactly."

She clicks her tongue. "It's fishy. Are you sure he's not married? Some of those guys in clubs take off their wedding rings, you know. Sneaky assholes."

I sit up straighter, anger itching just below the surface for all the cheated-on women everywhere. I'm part of their ranks now because of stupid Kyle.

"You think? What a dirty, rotten bastard." I rub my head, feeling a headache coming on. It's been building for a while. "You know when I first walked in, I thought I saw him with some skinny blonde, but then when we started talking in the hallway, I just assumed he was single. I'm so stupid. I mean, really? *An errand?"* I groan. "He probably had to go by diapers or baby formula before he went home."

Lulu sighs. "Mother trucker. Want me to kick his ass?"

My lips tighten and I sigh. "No, leave that to me, but we might have to go back to that bar tomorrow just to find him."

"I'll need to get a sitter for the dogs and Jean Claude, but I'm in."

We talk about what all we'll say to Mr. Cheater, but I know I'm just bluffing. I'm never going back to that bar. Tonight was a lesson: guys are a waste of my precious time. If I really need to get off, I can always pull out my battery-operated boyfriend. At least he doesn't lie to me.

I take another bite of ice cream. "Tonight was just a horrible idea."

Lulu sighs. "See you in the morning?"

I mumble a goodnight, set the phone down, and think, digging hard for my usual optimism. Tonight may have been a disaster, but tomorrow is a new day.

And my weekend can't get any worse.

THE RIGHT STUD

—

"Bacon! Bacon!" Rufus's scratchy voice greets me as I come down the stairs and enter the kitchen the next morning.

It's eight, and my eyes are barely open as I give the long-tailed, scarlet macaw a bleary glance. Like a regal king, he's perched on the top of an antique curio in the kitchen, one of the few spots I let him hang out when he's not in his cage. His beady, seemingly omniscient eyes follow me as I drag myself over to the kitchen counter.

"Coffee first, then bacon," I mutter as I pass. "Be glad I let you eat my pork at all, bird."

"Bacon!" he belts out as his head bobs back and forth.

I flip him off.

He gets the gist of my meaning, and it's confirmed when he shouts through the kitchen, "Fuck off! Fuck off!"

I roll my eyes and open the cabinet door to grab the coffee supplies just as Mrs. C waltzes in the room. I keep my face straight when I see her—like I do most days. Artsy and a bit of a kook, she's wearing yellow and blue plaid... pajamaralls?

"I like your outfit." It's a neutral term for the garish, flannel overalls that look like she could sleep in them.

"Thanks, dearie. No chafing, and I can fish in them!" she says in her thick southern accent as she swishes around the room. "Stop misbehavin', Rufus! I can hear your screeching all the way in my bedroom."

Mrs. C owns the obscene bird, and when she asked to be my first boarder, I ditched my "no pets" policy and jumped at the opportunity. Especially since she'd been a friend of Granny's, *and* she's paying me money I desperately need to renovate the house. Her gray hair is still in pink rollers, but she's in full makeup, ready to take on the day.

"Bacon!" Rufus cries.

We both ignore him.

"Did you sleep well?" I ask, pushing the start button on the coffee and busying myself with getting out the ingredients to make her favorite blueberry muffins.

I don't make a full breakfast during the week, but the weekends are all about the good food.

"Slept fine. How was your big night out? Did you meet someone nice?" Behind round spectacles, her eyes are gleaming, and I try to hide my grimace, hating to disappoint her after she'd been so enthusiastic when I left last night in my red dress.

"Meh. I don't think the nice ones hang out at the Smoky Siren." I force a smile following a long exhale. "You sit down and I'll make breakfast. It's what a B&B owner is supposed to do after all."

"Back in my day, they'd tell you to go to church to meet a nice man." Her eyebrow arches, and she leans closer. "I met Mr. C at the farmer's market, not that I'm knocking the Lord's house. I just think after a while, it helps to have something else in common. Once the poking phase wears off."

"Is that so…" I focus on cracking eggs into the dry mix and not encouraging her.

"The poking phase is necessary. Don't get me wrong, and I do enjoy the pleasures of the flesh." She taps her finger on the counter and her voice goes lower. "You'd never believe how stimulating fresh produce can be. Why I'd never seen a zucchini with such length… and girth. I grew a tomato once that looked just like a—"

"Did you know tomatoes are berries?" Sweet Baby Jesus, I

am not discussing erotic vegetables with Mrs. C!

"Of course." She pulls back, tugging her pajamarall straps. "Anyway, what do you like to do?"

Glancing at the bowl of yellow muffin batter mixed with dark purple blueberries, I consider her question. "I like to bake…"

"That's good. Men love women who bake."

"I like restoring furniture and fixing up this old house…"

"You're getting better at it, too." She gives me a pat on the back as she takes her usual seat at the rectangular table for eight, another one of Granny's antiques. "This table is gorgeous."

I smile. "Thank you."

I'd redone it this past month, stripping the polyurethane and stain off and then repainting it with a soft green chalk paint. A few hours with a sander and the end product is what I considered the masterpiece of the kitchen, a breezy shabby chic table with a distressed finish.

"And don't you worry," she continues as I slide the muffin tin into the oven. "I ain't had a man in twenty years, and I'm happy as can be. Sure I get lonely, but that's why I have Rufus to talk to. I tell him everything, even my ailments. Why just last week I was explaining to him the pain of having a hemorrhoid and I swear to God he was nodding his head in all the right spots. He gets me. Birds are fascinating. Did I ever tell you…"

She rambles on about the intelligence of Rufus, and I tune her out as I go to the fridge and pull out the spinach and cheese frittata I'd prepared yesterday. I set it on the counter and hustle around to the back door where I pull Granny's apron off the hook and slip it over my head, tying it in the back. White and soft with a couple of holes from being washed so many times, it's another part of the house I don't want to let go.

The muffins and frittata are baking and are close to being done as I fry the bacon for Rufus. I'm making about ten slices, my intent to stay caught up on his treats for the week.

Mrs. C is on her second cup of coffee and making a list of the items she wants me to pick up for her at the local art store when the doorbell rings.

"Can you get that?" I ask her. "It's either Ben or Lulu."

I strain my ears to hear the familiar barking of Lulu's entourage, but there's only silence coming from the foyer that leads to the front door. It's probably my brother Ben wanting to talk about selling the house—again.

Granny left this old place to both of us equally when she passed, and while I want to keep it as a home and a business, Ben wants to sell, with absolutely zero sense of nostalgia or family loyalty…

Familiar anger tightens my throat as I think about our disagreements these past weeks. We've always been close growing up, but this impasse is really pulling us apart.

Mrs. C pushes her glasses up on her nose as she rises. "Sure, dearie."

Careful to avoid the grease spatters, I use a fork to extract the bacon from the cast-iron skillet just as I hear a male voice down the hall along with Mrs. C's loud laugh.

Hmm, must be Ben, although he's not one to make Mrs. C laugh.

I square my shoulders, preparing for defense, as I pat down a piece of bacon to get off the excess grease.

"Bacon! Fuck!" Rufus' head bobs back and forth as he watches me blow on the pork.

I hold it up for him just out of reach, chastising him. "You're a crazy ass bird, you know that?"

I toss it up in the air, and he catches it with his beak. Using his claws, he delicately plucks it apart. His eyes send me a thank you—or so I tell myself. I briefly wonder if his bacon addiction is going to put him in an early parrot grave—but I forget everything when Mrs. C and the man who definitely isn't Ben walk into the kitchen.

Oh. My. God. Random Hot Guy stares at me, and the humiliation of last night, of waiting for him for two hours, flies over me.

My lips press into a frown and I put my hands on my hips. "What the hell are you doing here?"

Chapter 4

Jax

I pull up to The Conch Shell and take it in. It sits on a small rise facing the ocean, surrounded by grass and sand. A beautiful, rambling two-story Victorian-style home with a front porch that looks straight out of *Southern Living*, the exterior is painted a bright azure color, faded and peeling in places. My eye catches a fallen board on the bottom right side. Still, the front door is a freshly painted stark white, slightly distressed, a sure sign that someone is attempting to slowly redo the place.

I study it critically as I walk to the side of the house, taking in the structure and bones. Technically, my meeting with the owner isn't until ten, but I'd come out a bit early to get the lay of the land. Also, I'd anticipated more summer traffic as I drove in from Charleston, but the roads had been clear.

The wooden accents in the corner of the porch show signs of dry rot. The entire house I'm sure is a maintenance nightmare—a wooden house in a perpetually damp climate. Behind me, the ocean crashes, and I turn to look out at the sea. But damn, that's a stunning view. I can only imagine the owners got it for a song, decades before the area became such coveted real estate. It makes sense to fix it up...

Or sell it.

The developer side of me rears its mercenary head, the part that had Pearson's Real Estate Developers, Inc., recruiting me out of architecture school to exploit. My eye for investment, for cultivating traffic flow and increasing commercial appeal are all elements of design I learned from my dad, from the years we'd spent in the hot sun building houses while he shared with me his dream of designing them.

When he was young, he didn't have the money to go to school, and then he died before he ever had a chance to go back. Going to architecture school was the one thing I wanted to do to honor his memory.

I pull out my phone and take a few snaps of the problematic areas. If this restoration angle doesn't work out, maybe the old lady will be interested in making a few million. I've never met a woman I couldn't charm out of her real estate... among other things.

Strolling to the front door, I slide my phone into my breast pocket and press the white button centered in a plate that appears hand-painted with seashells and a little mermaid. I've got to hand it to the decorator—she's a true artist.

The door flies open, and I straighten. Then I almost laugh at the short round elderly lady eying me with suspicion. She's wearing bright yellow, flannel overalls, and after a second of scrutiny, her gray brows arch, a scheming light hitting her eye.

"Well, hello! And you are?"

"Jax." I extend a hand. "Jax Roland. You must be Ms. Hall. I'm here early—I apologize. I left my suitcase is in the car. We can look around first if my room isn't ready yet."

"A new boarder!" She claps and steps to the side, motioning for me to enter. "Right this way, kind sir."

I'm confused by her *new boarder* comment, since she invited me to stay. The foyer is part of an open floor plan, and a deep red Persian rug connects it to the living area. Oak paneling covers the walls, which I don't like. It would look better with some shiplap or just a coat of paint over it. Maybe textured? I'm already taking mental notes of things I'd change if this place was mine. Tall windows flood the space with light, which is fantastic, pulling the eye out to the beach beyond.

I follow her through the hall into a sitting room, complete with a smoke-stained fireplace, Edwardian armchairs, and a gold velvet sofa with tapestry pillows. A black baby grand toped with lace doilies and black and white framed photos sits in the corner of the room near the window. It is definitely an old lady place.

"Like I said, I'm sorry if I'm early…" I stop talking, since she clearly isn't listening as she bustles off ahead of me like she's running from a fire.

She waves a hand over her head as she continues down the hall in the opposite direction, and the intoxicating aroma of fresh bacon laced with sweet blueberries floats in the air. My stomach growls, and I follow her to what must be the kitchen.

"Tell me," she says as she looks at me from over her shoulder, "Do you like fresh produce, Jax Roland?"

What an odd question, but I'm about to answer when the entry way opens on a bright room, and my jaw drops. Standing in front of a stainless range with her dark hair swept up in a messy bun and her long, silky legs extending from behind a tattered white apron is the girl from the Smoky Siren. *Ashton.*

Her eyes flare as they rake over me, taking in my navy shirt, jeans, and leather loafers. Her mouth tightens. Obviously, she's not happy to see me.

"What the hell are you doing here?" she snaps.

I'm reeling. "What the fu-udge?" I manage to keep it civil,

but just barely.

The gorgeous sex kitten with lips like heaven is standing right in front of me or at least her really pissed off identical twin sister... who's still pretty gorgeous, despite the anger blazing in her eyes.

"I, uh... I'm not sure what's happening right now." I look from her to the older woman totally confused.

"Ashton Hall"—the old woman waves her hand between us —"this is Jax Roland. He says he's here to stay."

"*You're* Ms. Hall? The lady who contacted me about renovating a beach house?" Our eyes lock. Mine I'm sure are confused as shit, while hers are brownish-green firecrackers.

"And you're Jax Roland." Her anger is still there, but it's changing into something like furious embarrassment, turning her cheeks a pretty pink.

She looks down, wipes her hand on the white apron, and quickly slips it over her head. "You're early. I'm not ready for our meeting."

She's dressed in cutoffs and a tight tee, and my eyes travel quickly down her perfect legs to her cute little bare feet where her toenails are painted red, the same color as her dress last night.

"I'm sorry." I clear my throat. "I expected the traffic to be heavier, and I wanted to get a feel for the place before we started."

A buzzer sounds, and she spins around, leaning forward to open the oven, filling the small kitchen with the mouthwatering aroma of what looks like some kind of breakfast pie and blueberry muffins. The scent combined with the sight of that ass straining toward me in cutoffs...

"Jesus," I hiss softly, and I hear a chuckle to my left. Averting my eyes from Ashton, I catch the old woman grinning, and I know I'm busted having impure thoughts.

The oven door slams, and Ashton drops two pans on the stone-tile countertop, her movements agile and confident as if she's done this a thousand times. She's still not facing me as she bustles around the kitchen, opening cabinets and yanking out dishes.

I dart my eyes over at the older lady, but she's watching us both with a smirk.

"Um, can I help you with anything?" I ask.

"You could start by being on time. It seems you have a problem with keeping track of your commitments, Mr. Roland."

Ah, she means last night…

When she turns around, her hand is on her hip. "If you'll give me a few minutes."

"Take all the time you need—" I start, but she cuts me off.

"I'll be ready at ten, like I said I would." Her eyes flash as she adds the last part. "Help yourself to breakfast. Everything you need is right here." She indicates the area on the buffet where she's set up plates, silverware, and napkins, then nods at the counter space next to the fridge. "OJ and coffee are over there."

"I don't mean to disrupt. I can always leave and come back —"

"Don't be ridiculous." She slaps down an oven mitt. "You're here. You must eat something."

She storms out of the kitchen without another word, and the old woman steps forward, picking up one of the stacked plates. "That girl is a great baker. Sassy to."

Yeah.

My eyes are fixed on the space where Ashton Hall stood

while I try to decide if I should curse my shitty timing or thank my lucky stars.

When I finally got back to the Smoky Siren last night, it was dark and locked up tight, and I was sure I'd never see Ashton again. I figured it was karma for lying to my date for the evening.

The reason for my late arrival to the bar was my sister's frantic phone call that her cat was stuck on the roof. I told her it would climb down on its own, but no, her three kids were crying and apparently Mittens would die up there alone all night...

I wound up climbing a ladder in my suit and searching through the fucking tree limbs leaning over her roof—which I informed her she needs to trim today—until I found a fluffy white kitten that bit me as a thank you.

"You never told me how you feel about fresh produce." The old lady loads a plate with frittata, three muffins, and five strips of bacon and hands it to me.

"Thanks." Shaking my head, I take the overflowing dish, not really sure what to do next. "I had breakfast at the hotel."

"Powdered eggs and bruised oranges. Am I right?" She's stacking her own plate, and I can't argue with her.

"I had a protein bar." I set my plate on the table where she's now sitting.

"Might as well have eaten a Snickers."

I pour myself a cup of coffee, dousing it with the heavy cream sitting beside the pot. As I make my way to the table and pull out a chair, the older lady is eyeing me critically, and I feel like she's taking notes.

I take a seat and she starts in. "Are you married?" She chews on a piece of muffin. "My name's Mona Capshaw, by the way, but most people call me Mrs. C."

I huff out a laugh. "Nice to meet you, Mrs. C, and no, I've never been married. You?"

She laughs. "My man's been gone for years, but boy did we have some good times. Like Ashton, he loved to cook." She gets a wistful expression on her face. "My favorite dish was these stuffed peppers. He'd take fresh jalapeños and cut them in half, fill them with shrimp and cream cheese, top with breadcrumbs and bake at 450… Mmm…" She presses her lips together, then immediately arches an eyebrow. "Just be sure to wash your hands after handling the peppers. Mr. C forgot once, and well, let's just say my more delicate parts weren't happy."

I nearly choke on the coffee I just swallowed. "Noted." I quickly bite into a golden muffin and lean back in my chair as buttery, blueberry goodness fills my mouth. "Damn…"

"Told ya that girl can bake." She follows suit, and I'm busy scarfing down the rest, glad I have two more. "It's one of her many talents. Handyman work is not one of them, although she does a great job restoring old furniture. Take this table for instance."

"Nice craftsmanship." I slide my hand over the soft finish.

"Took her mind off that good-for-nothing fiancé, not that you heard it from me…"

"Fuck! Bacon!" The voice is loud and scratchy and right behind me, as a large bird snatches one of the five bacon strips off my plate, nearly taking a finger with him.

"What the hell?" I sit back with a jerk, and the old lady rises fast. I don't know how I missed the bird when I came in, but there it is. "Excuse my French."

"Rufus! Don't be an asshole!" She sweeps him away and he flies back to a tall curio where he perches and eats his prize. She pats my shoulder. "Don't apologize. It's why I gave you extra bacon. That feathered freak has no manners, but he is a good listener."

"He belongs to you?"

"Yep." She strokes his blue head, and the bird nods repeatedly. "Got him as a little fellow. Didn't realize he'd outlive me." She chuckles softly. "I'm stuck with him now."

I rise, taking my empty plate. "You done?"

Mrs. C nods, and I carry hers to the sink as well when Ashton breezes into the room again. My back straightens, and I follow her with my eyes. She's all business, dressed in cropped white linen pants and a simple summer shirt. Her lips are pale pink, and her long hair is brushed back in a tight ponytail. I'm already missing the easy breezy girl cooking in cutoffs.

She looks me up and down. "Are you ready to get started?"

"I'm ready when you are."

I follow her out the door. She's doing her best to let me know she's not interested. I'd buy it if it weren't for that kiss we shared. Her cute little ass is perfect even in linen pants, and if I can't salvage this old place, I'm determined to salvage last night.

Chapter 5

Ashton

Holding my notebook in my hands, I do my best to focus on the list and not sexy Jax Roland, who by the way looks nothing like he does on *The Right Stud*, where he's always wearing a Dallas Cowboys ball cap pulled low and a thick scruff on his cheeks. Sometimes he dons thick, plastic goggles when he's being manly and tearing down a wall or something, or a ventilation mask if he's worried about asbestos.

I'd recently come across his YouTube channel when I was researching how to install a backsplash, and I admit, watching his fine ass in his tight jeans had been mesmerizing—which would explain why he seemed familiar last night. I should have recognized his voice, only I wasn't expecting to lock lips with *The Right Stud* at the Smoky Siren.

About a month ago, he mentioned on one of his shows that he grew up in the Charleston area, and he'd love to redo a beach house. My idea immediately took shape.

Why not invite him out and see if he'd be interested in doing some of my rehab for his show? It would be a great way to create buzz about my B&B while also getting an expert to give me ideas and possibly do the repairs at a discount. I'd even offered to let him stay here while he worked.

He agreed, and here we are.

Only he's a sneaky bastard. Lulu's argument is reinforced even more by his sudden change of appearance. I am not getting mixed up with another guy leading a double life, no matter how panty-melting his kisses are... or how shiny his hair is in the sunlight... or how intense his blue gaze is on me.

As if he knows what I'm thinking, he says, "Before we go any further, I'm sorry about last night."

My lips tighten, and I swallow down a snarky comeback. "It's fine. I hung out with my friend Roger. He was nice."

His jaw tightens. "I bet he was."

I brush nonexistent lint off the hem of my shirt, ignoring the fact that he seems a little jealous. "You said you'd be back, and you never were. You lied." I let out a sigh. "I don't waste time on men who lie, Mr. Roland—"

"Please, call me Jax, and it wasn't a lie. I had to rescue my niece's cat from a tree."

"Your niece's cat." I give him a *get real* look. "Is that so?"

He nods. "If you knew my crazy family, you'd understand. My sister has three kids, triplet girls, and something always goes wrong."

I arch a brow. "And she doesn't have a husband who can rescue kittens?"

"He's out of town. Business trip."

"How convenient." It's almost impossible not to roll my eyes. "Let me get this straight. You didn't come back because you had to climb a tree and rescue a poor animal—not because you were actually at the Smoky Siren with someone else and left with her and then decided to ditch me?"

I'm just spit-balling here, but I'm pretty sure I saw him leaving at the same time as a skinny blonde. I hadn't wanted to believe it. I don't want to believe it now. And yet...

A flash of regret passes over his face and he chews on his bottom lip. "Well... I actually was there with someone. But, in my defense, it was a setup. I did *not* want to be with her. You walked in, and—"

Shit.

Dammit.

Dammit dammit!

"Stop!" I hold my hands up. "No need to explain any further. Let's just forget last night and focus on today." Sadly, I'd been right, and he's an ass who was with someone. It doesn't matter, because right now this house is my priority. Pointing with my pencil, I squint into the sun. "Everything started when we replaced the roof last year."

He studies me intently as if wanting to continue explaining his actions, but after a moment he gives up and follows my lead.

He looks up at the top of the house. "Okay... and why did you replace it?"

"Some salesman talked Granny into installing a cedar shake roof. He said it would add to the original Chesapeake-style design of the home."

Jax's brow furrows. "Add to the overall dry rot you mean. Cedar shake in this climate? You might as well put a giant sponge up there. Was it ever dry?"

"It lasted about five years... and caused thousands in damage."

"You should sue that guy."

I confess, his defensiveness is encouraging. "He disappeared. Moved back to Arizona or Las Vegas. Anyway, we replaced it with a Ridgeline roof, using Hardie board as a base to keep out the moisture."

He lets out a low whistle. "That must've set you back quite a bit."

"We had to do it." My voice is quiet as I cringe inwardly at the mountain of debt hanging over my head, from the new roof to my failed wedding. It's just more fuel for Ben's argument to sell the home. "I hope I can save money on the rest of the work... if possible."

Jax lips tighten into a straight line. "What else is on your list?"

"Most of it was caused by the water damage from the roof..." Walking up to the wraparound porch, I show him the rotting accents, the corbels and molding that need to be replaced.

He follows me, I assume taking mental notes.

"Watch where you step here or you'll crash through." I guide him around the rotten planks in the floor, and I nearly jump out of my skin at Mrs. C standing inside one of the open windows.

"Don't forget the critters in the crawl space!" she yells.

"Critters?" Jax's frown deepens.

He's done nothing but frown the entire tour, making me feel sicker and sicker.

Exhaling a laugh, I wave my hand. "It's just some local wildlife—"

"It's a family of skunks!" Mrs. C adds.

My face flames red, and I try to hurry us along the wrap-around porch away from our stalker. "Don't mind her, that's not on my list to show you."

"It should be on your list to show somebody!" she shouts after us.

Jax stops and crosses his arms over his chest. The navy tee he's wearing stretches taut, and I can't help gazing at his bulging biceps.

Everything about him is solid, and I remember the feel of his hard chest against my soft body in the hall last night. It sends crazy tingles through my lower stomach.

His voice is stern, making the tingles even hotter. "If it *is* skunks, and they set up shop, the whole house will be intolerable."

I bite my lip. I'm not sure why I'm so embarrassed by the skunk family. It's not like I sent them a printed invitation to move in. "We're not certain they're skunks—"

"Yes, we are!" Mrs. C cries. I want to strangle her.

Jax bends down and looks through one of the holes in the planks. "You'll have to lure them out then install lattice or chicken wire to keep them from getting back into their den. If they have kits—"

His voice is drowned out by a blast of barking dogs followed by the sound of Lulu shouting, "Hello, everyone!"

"Oh, what next?" I mutter, stepping carefully to the porch railing and waving to my best friend.

Her red hair is flying around her head in crazy spirals as she walks five dogs up the sandy lane—or are they walking her? It's hard to tell with the way she half-runs behind them. The mutts range in size from a small Chihuahua mix to a pretty collie that reminds me of Lassie.

"I'm here on the promise of muffins!" She waves at us, smiling as she approaches. Her eyes land on Jax and widen then fly back to me. "I didn't know you had company?"

"It's the home improvement guy I was telling you about. The one who's going to be staying here."

She's at the bottom of the porch now, tying the leashes up to a special post I set up just for her, complete with a few large bowls of water. "Oh, Hi."

Jax sends her a wave, a small smile on his face. "Jax Roland. *The Right Stud.*"

Lulu's eyebrows shoot straight up. "If you do say so yourself."

He laughs. "Yeah, it's a fun name. You have to be memorable if you want to make it to the big leagues."

"You got my attention," Lulu murmurs, coming up the stairs to join us. She rakes her green eyes over him, I'm sure taking in the styled blond hair and chiseled jawline. "I'm Lulu, Ashton's best friend. She tells me everything—although, she left out how hot you are."

I clear my throat. "He's also the guy from the Smoky Siren last night."

Lulu rears back. "Oh, shit. You screwed that up."

Exactly.

Jax's face reddens. "I can explain—"

Waving my hand, I cut him off and motion for her to go inside. "We're just finishing up the tour. I've already set out breakfast in the kitchen if you want to head inside."

"I'd rather hang out here and get to know Jax." She's got a twinkle in her eye that I know means she's up to mischief. "So you carry a hammer? Any relation to Thor?"

"Good one, Lu!" Mrs. C calls through the screen.

"Different type of hammer." Jax doesn't miss a beat. "So... no."

"I see." My friend's eyes narrow. "And are you married? Did you leave the bar to buy baby formula last night?"

Jax does a slow blink. "No."

Lulu chews on her lip, her gaze lasered in on him. "You know what? I believe you."

Good lord. Between her and Mrs. C, I can't even have a

conversation with him about the house.

"Lulu, we really need to finish here, and I'm sure this is terribly boring to you—"

"I'm not bored in the least—" she starts.

"Go inside. Please." I flare my eyes at her and she seems to get it, because she lets out a little sigh of disappointment.

"Fine." She flips around and tosses a final look in Jax's direction. "Nice to meet you, Mr. *Right Stud*. I can't wait to get to know you better."

Turning to Jax, my chest is tight as I wait for the verdict. "Sorry about that."

"Nothing I'm not used to. Is that everything on your list?"

Glancing down at my notebook, I do a little shrug. "The only things left are just minor interior fixes. A few of the spokes on the bannister are wobbly. One of the bathrooms needs a mini-makeover—the one in your bedroom as a matter of fact. We call it the haunted bathroom." His brow lowers, and I try to hurry past my slip. "Maybe we can just leave it for character."

"What makes it haunted?"

"Uh… the lights flicker at odd, random times. I've changed the bulbs, but nothing seems to work." I glance up, and he's still making that super-focused, stern face. It's actually kind of sexy.

"Sounds like an electrical problem. If you leave it, it could cause a fire. Burn the entire house down."

"Oh, my lord!" My stomach tightens more. Electricians are almost as expensive as roofers.

Letting out a sigh, he shoves his hands in his back pockets and looks over the place. I'm not sure I can breathe waiting for what he's about to say.

"What do you think?" My voice is small. "Is this something that would work for your show?"

The muscle in his square jaw moves before he answers, and my heart sinks as I brace for his rejection.

"It's the absolute worst style of house for a damp climate like this. You'll always be keeping up with repairs." He holds his hands up as if he's framing the house in a camera. "Still, it's a gorgeous view, and for a home repair show, it's kind of perfect. Lots of common but interesting projects for the viewers. I can picture it now, a golden sunset on the Atlantic with your house in the background. It will be fantastic." He looks back at me with his hands still up, putting me in his frame. "Having a beautiful girl like you as the owner adds to the charm." Dropping his hands, he grins sheepishly. "Sorry. I'm not flirting, and I hope you're not offended. Just stating a fact. My viewers will adore you."

His gaze lingers on my face, and I feel myself blushing. "You really think so?"

He nods. "I think you and your house are perfect for my show."

For the first time in weeks, pure joy fills me. Without thinking, I jump forward, throwing my arms around his neck and giving him the biggest hug. "Oh, thank you!"

His chest is a solid wall of steel and he smells divine, like sandalwood and citrus. Warm hands slide down to my waist, and my stomach flutters.

I step back quickly, twisting my hands in front of me. "I'm sorry. That was totally unprofessional. I'll never do it again."

My eyes are fixed on his beach-style loafers, which are definitely not the look of a handyman, but I get it. He's got two sides: Mr. Suit and Mr. Stud. I imagine him working on my porch, sweating in the South Carolina sun with a hammer in his hand... Thor's got nothing on *The Right Stud.*

He cuts through my daydream with a laugh. "It's okay. Enthusiasm is vital for big jobs. It's a great response, especially for when we have a spectacular finish."

My face flames at the thought of finishing spectacularly with him, and I cough to cover my swoon. He clears his throat, and when our eyes catch, I'm pretty sure he was thinking the same thing I was.

He's quickly back to business. "Let me run the numbers for the repairs and see what we're up against."

"Thank you. I can't even express how happy I am that you're interested."

He nods. "And about last night—"

I wave him off. "Let's just forget it ever happened. Clean slate. I had a few drinks and acted out of character. Anyway, it's not like it can ever happen again, since we're working together." My laugh sounds nervous, and I inhale deeply. "What I meant is, I'm not looking for anything serious right now, but I'm looking forward to our business relationship—as friends."

He frowns but then nods. "Okay."

I've got to get out of here before I say something ridiculous. "Let me show you to your room."

Chapter 6

Ashton

Jax stops to grab a suitcase from the trunk of his grey Audi S8, and I lead him up the staircase to the second level. After a brief tour of the sitting room, with its huge window overlooking the shore, I lead him to the suite on the east side of the house.

"Mine is on the opposite end." I point down the long hallway. I'm already sweating thinking about him sleeping just down the hall from me.

"Ah, you've got the sunset view."

"It's my favorite room." When I was younger, my grand-mother had decorated it for me in a sea theme with starfish and mermaids. I've never had the heart to update it.

"Your room is east, but the windows face the beach, which is south."

"No early morning sun in the face?" he laughs.

"Right."

Opening the door, I show him the nautical-themed room I updated myself. A plush navy-checked duvet covers the queen size bed placed underneath a wide window with a view of the beach. An anchor rug is on the hardwood floors, tying everything together.

"Nice bed," he says, and I blink, picturing him naked and

rolling around with me in it.

I clear my throat and show him the bathroom. Thankfully, the light is working when I flick it on. The toilet is oddly silent too.

I laugh and look over at him. "Looks like the ghosts don't mind you staying here."

He grins. "I'll investigate and fix it for you."

My insides warm. I bet he can fix more than a light...

Ashton! Stop daydreaming. For the sake of all scorned women, leave him be!

I follow him back into the bedroom. "Where do the bird and Mrs. C stay?" he asks.

"They have a room on the main floor. Sometimes she has trouble with her knees, so it's easier on her."

"So you and I are the only ones up here?"

"For the moment." I struggle to hold back more visions of the two of us up here, all alone.

"How many bedrooms total?"

"Six. Yours, mine, and Mrs. C's all have private baths. The other three share a communal bathroom. I also had a powder room installed downstairs when I first moved in."

He nods, thinking. "It's a great setup. I'm really digging it."

I grin like a schoolgirl. I love that someone else shares my affection for this old house. "Once you're settled in, I can show you the widow's walk on the third floor. It's so cool."

His eyes light up. "I'd love that."

I go to the door. "I'll leave you alone to work the numbers. I can't wait to hear your thoughts... about working together."

"I'm looking forward to it." His blue eyes are on me intently, and I think I recognize that look—it's definitely interest.

"Okay." I kind of want to stay, but he probably needs to

decompress.

The desire to linger is squashed by a shout from downstairs. "Ashton! Where are you?" It echoes throughout the whole house.

Jax's brow furrows, and I realize my apprehension must be showing on my face. "Who is that?"

"It's only my brother." I hurry out, into the hall. "Go ahead and take your time. We can talk more later."

The last thing I want is for Jax to hear what Ben thinks of my restoration plans. Jogging downstairs, I stop in the foyer, facing my guest.

Ben is handsome, tall with wavy brown hair and brown eyes. As a thirty-five year-old confirmed bachelor, he's built a successful law practice and a small fortune. His motto: If it's not making money, sell it. It's why we argue constantly over Granny's house.

"Good morning," I say, kissing his cheek. "Are you hungry? I have blueberry muffins and frittata. Rufus has probably eaten all the bacon, but I can fry more if you want."

"I already ate, thanks." His tone is impatient. Again. "Have you thought any more about what I said?"

"Yes," I say sharply. "And you'll be interested to know I've just finished showing the place to the host of a national home improvement show."

"Oh really?" He doesn't seem as impressed as I'd hoped. "Which one?"

We step into the sitting room, beside Granny's doily-covered piano. "It's called *The Right Stud*. They're considering putting us on their show."

"*The Right Stud*?" Ben's brow furrows. "Never heard of it."

"Well, either way, it has a huge following. The host is here now running the numbers and putting together a plan to make this place famous."

"Ashton, seriously. Why are you wasting time and energy on a money pit when we can sell it for millions and split the profits?"

My heart drops. "Because it's our family home, and it's not wasting anything. Being on the show means I can get the repairs done cheaply, and the publicity will send tourists flocking to us. Wouldn't you rather have an ongoing investment instead of a one-time payout?"

Ben sighs. "You're being optimistic. Running this place is work. The maintenance is a nightmare. Granny could never keep up with it all."

"I can do it."

"Why would you want to?" He frowns, and his eyes trace around the living room. "It's an antiquated dump."

My fists tighten. "It is not a dump. The Conch Shell is all I have right now, and I'd appreciate it if you'd show it some respect."

"Look, I'm sorry things didn't work out with Kyle, but that's no reason to be blind to the fact that this house is worth more sold than restored."

My hands are on my hips. "I will never believe that."

"Okay…" Ben rakes a hand over his jaw. He scans the room again, then walks toward the foyer, where he stops and places both hands on his hips. "I'll make a deal with you. I'll run the listing past some people I know"—he lifts his chin toward the second floor—"you find out what this stud-guy says. We'll compare notes and see which makes more financial sense. Deal?"

Dread unfurls in my gut. It's not like I can say no. Half of this house belongs to Ben. He just doesn't love it like I do, and

I'm in no position to offer to buy him out of his share—not with the mountain of debt I've recently accumulated.

"I guess."

"Great. I'll get a developer out here ASAP."

I frown. "Wait. A developer? I thought you meant someone who wanted to buy it."

"The land is worth more than the house. A developer will buy it, clear the lot, and sell it to someone who'll build high-rise condos."

I think I'm going to be sick. "Clear the lot... that means tear the house down."

Ben pats me on the arm. "Just think about what you could do with all that money. You could open a bakery if you wanted."

I bite my lip. "I like baking *here,* in Granny's house, for my guests."

The moment is defused when Lulu breezes into the room. Her eyes land on Ben, and she goes straight to him. "I thought I heard your voice. Want a muffin?"

Her eyelashes flutter, and she presents a small plate holding three of my fresh-baked goodies.

He takes one and pops a piece in his mouth. "Thanks, babe. I saw your dogs outside."

My best friend's cheeks flush at his casual *babe*. She's had a crush on my brother since we were kids with skinned knees and pigtails. Now that he's single again, she's back to waving that torch she's been carrying for a hundred years.

My brother has always seemed completely oblivious to her obsession, but he seems to be giving her more attention these days.

"You coming into the office today?" he asks, heading for the door. "I have some divorce papers for you to serve, and you know they never expect it on a Saturday."

Her auburn brow arches, and her frustrated inner-actress emerges. "Is it a Kardashian or a Larry the Cable Guy situation?"

Ben actually laughs. "More like a zoo keeper. It seems the husband likes dressing up in those team mascot outfits and having sex with other... female mascots?"

"Whaaat?" Lulu's green eyes sparkle, and I see she's in planning mode. "This has all kinds of possibilities. I have a delivery-guy uniform that can double as animal control, and of course, there's my Easter bunny disguise..."

She'd used that one to serve a guy who'd been robbing vending machines around town. It's a Playboy bunny base with oversized, cartoonish hands and feet.

"You've got to think creatively," Lulu winks.

My brother's eyes flicker up and down my best friend's body. "I'm pretty creative, but I'll be interested to see how you handle it."

Hold the phone. *Did Ben just flirt with Lulu?*

I didn't think my best friend's cheeks could get any pinker, but she manages a purr. "Well, this bunny is ready to play."

"I look forward to seeing her again." Ben winks and heads out the door. "Be in the office in an hour?"

"You know it."

He's gone, and Lulu collapses against the bannister, clutching her chest. "Did that just happen?"

"I'm not sure, but something happened. If I weren't so mad at him right now, I might be excited for you."

"It's that bunny costume. Works every time."

"How so?"

"Men are so dazzled by the sight of cleavage, they forget everything else." She looks down at her denim overalls and bright green Converse high-tops. "Why did I leave the house dressed like this?"

"Because it's your job. You have fifty dogs walking you every day."

"Five dogs," she corrects, frowning into the round mirror hanging on the wall and smoothing her curls. "I had a feeling I should've worn a dress. I didn't even fix my hair."

"I can't believe you of all people ignored your instincts."

In addition to being Palmetto's most creative process server, my best friend also does tarot readings out of her house, which is also her dog-walking and pet-grooming business.

"What was he doing here anyway? How dare he surprise me like this!"

The memory of his words forces a little growl from me. "He was giving me a hard time about the house again."

"Oh, he'll come around." Lulu walks around the room, visibly buzzing from my older brother's attention. "He's already warming up, it seems. I've got to get home and change."

Shaking my head, I pick up the small plate still holding a muffin. "I don't know how you do it. You know people hate process servers, right? They're probably calling you bad names behind your back."

That snaps her out of her lust-induced haze. "How can anyone call the Easter bunny bad names?"

"Pretty easily, I'd imagine."

"That's where you're wrong. These people are criminals, Ashton." She emphasizes the word *criminals*. "I'm the best at what I do because I take the sting out of them paying their debt to society."

"So what? You're Mary Poppins now?"

"Only in that I also have magical abilities." She follows me to the kitchen. "I've got to get the dogs home. Is it okay if I leave Jean Claude here for now? He chewed through the fence last night, and I haven't had time to fix it."

"No—Lulu!" I slam the plate on the counter a little too hard. "I don't want that goat on the property. He's stinky. He's a menace, and he's a bottomless pit. He ate all my azaleas last week, then he tried to eat all my hydrangeas."

"First, Jean Claude is a ram, hence his name, Jean Claude *van Ram*. Second, I tied him far away from all your precious flowers this time. He's practically in the ocean."

"Jean Claude is a goat, and male goats are not rams, they're billies."

"I can't call him Jean Claude *van Billy*."

"You *can* take his billy butt home."

But she's in front of me now, tugging on my arms. "Please let him stay, Ashton. This is the most interested Ben's ever seemed. It could finally be my chance."

I let out an exasperated growl. "Well, hurry up. I really need some time alone to think." The thought of a developer tearing down Granny's house has me feeling nauseated and wanting to cry.

"You should talk to JC about it."

"Jesus Christ?" I exhale a sigh. "I've never been much on religion but I suppose praying can't hurt."

"Jean Claude! He's an excellent emotional support animal. Just don't let him eat your hair."

Shaking my head, I follow her out the door. "I'd rather not talk to an animal with crazy eyes."

"I won't tell him you said that. Give me three hours, and I'll pick him up. I promise."

"I'll give you two."

Chapter 7

Jax

"I love the idea, but we don't have the budget. You're talking at least twenty thousand to cover supplies, a small crew, expenses, and incidentals." I can hear my producer Tara's fingers clicking on her keyboard through the phone.

"We can't get a sponsor?"

"I'm sure we can get YellaWood to cover the lumber supply. Last week's video got a million views, which is fantastic. Still, you need nails, glue… Your crew has to eat."

"I'll need a sander for the floor."

She breathes loudly in my ear. "I'm not a miracle worker, Jax. The networks practically have the market cornered on building supply sponsorships."

"Any word from Celia on that?" I step to the window and look down at the clear-blue breakers eating up the brown sand.

Celia is Tara's contact at HGTV. If she can get them to pick up *The Right Stud*, we won't have to worry about things like budgets and covering the cost of materials. They'll provide it all, including top-notch cameramen, editing, and post-production.

I could finally give Pearson's Real Estate Developers, Inc., my letter of resignation.

"Nada." She's quiet a moment, and I know she's number-crunching. "Okay, if you forego a cameraman and crew, it'll save enough to cover the remaining supplies. Provided nothing new pops up."

My jaw tightens. "I know. Something new always pops up."

Scrubbing my fingers against my forehead, I consider turning down this job when Ashton appears on the sandy path below. She's still wearing those cropped linen pants, but her shirt is untucked. Her hair is loose, blowing in long dark waves in the breeze, and her feet are once again bare.

Damn, she's pretty. When she hugged me today, pressing her soft tits against my chest, all I could think of was kissing her lips, her hot little body rocking into mine... I had to conjure images of Margaret Thatcher... or Mrs. C lurking in the window... or Rufus biting my finger off to keep the rise out of my pants.

I know from our emails she doesn't have the money to do the work this old place needs. It's the whole reason she invited me here in the first place. I'm not going to let her down. I'm doing this job.

Still, I can't deny the fact money is a necessary component. "It would help to have an extra twenty grand handy," I mutter.

"Oh, I know—just convert some native forestland into a Bass Pro Shops again." The sarcasm in Tara's voice makes me frown. She doesn't like my day job, obviously.

"It was unusable land. The trees were trash. If I hadn't closed the deal, someone else would have. That town was practically paying us for the development. I made a shit ton of money on that sale."

"Whatever helps you sleep at night."

My producer is a tree-hugging nitwit. "Look, I'm not defending my job to you. I care about the earth. I also care about paying my bills."

"And what will you leave your grandchildren?"

"A mountain of cash if I'm lucky." I've had enough of this conversation. I've got what I need. "Just be ready when I start sending you video. I want it to be a miniseries, a 'This Old Beach House' type of thing."

"What's the name of this old beach house?"

"The Conch Shell. It's very old lady, lace and doilies right now, but when we're done, it'll be polished and modern."

"Can't wait to see what you do."

We end the call, and I sit down at the small desk near the bed and pull out my laptop. Within a few minutes, I've got my 3-D design program up, and I'm entering the measurements I took earlier as I explored the rambling house.

Feeling inspired, I recreate the sitting room downstairs on my program, only this time I change the furniture to pieces that are light and airy. I add shiplap walls and newly sanded hardwood floors. It really isn't part of the renovation Ashton and I talked about, but I'm looking forward to showing it to her.

It's going to be more money, my head says.

Whatever. Maybe I won't even show it to her, but I have to admit her enthusiasm tugs at my heart. I know this house is important to her. Maybe I can find a way to add special touches to it…

After a few minutes of playing with the program, I stand and stretch, rolling my neck as I walk over to the window, where my eyes land on Ashton. She's now sitting on the sand with her knees bent, her back to what looks like a goat tied to a wooden fence. I can't help wondering how I missed *that* guy on the walking tour. I've never seen so much wildlife in one place before. Hell, it's practically a zoo.

Her forehead lowers to her arms, and her shoulders droop. She's visibly unhappy about something, and my chest tightens unexpectedly. I don't like seeing her this way. I want to jog down and tell her the good news when my phone lights up with a text.

It's from Blaine Pearson, my boss and the owner of the company. Must be something big. My mind goes to that Bass Pro deal I closed last year. It was the biggest of my career, and it netted us all several grand. Too bad living in Manhattan ain't cheap.

Got a lead on some beachfront property near Charleston. Isn't that where you are? Motivated seller and top-notch location. Incredible views. Could probably get it low and convert it high. Will send the address if you're interested?

Hmm. Selling takes time, and I want to focus all my attention on Ashton and this job. I send a quick reply. *I'm in the area but not working. I need this vacay.*

He answers like he already knew what I was going to say. *The commission might be six figures. Guess I'll pass it over to Joey. Have fun.*

Smartass. He knows I can't stand jerk-face Joey beating me out on a sweet deal. I think about the cash it would add to my back account. I could put more money into the show—buy new cameras, hire a cameraman for this job… Shit, with six figures, the possibilities are endless.

The ambitious side of me rises up—the shark, the closer. This sale is mine, and if the property is near Charleston, it would be stupid to say no. I'll just pop over and give it a look-see and then come right back here. Done.

I text back. *Okay. Send me the info, and I'll check it out.*

He texts me a number, and without hesitation, I tap it. The

phone rings and rings until I get voicemail.

"Hi, this is Jax Roland with Pearson Real Estate. I'm in the area, and I wanted to touch base about the property you're looking to sell. Give me a call at this number, and we can set up a meeting."

I leave my number and toss my phone on the dresser. Contact made, now I'm ready to get comfortable and dig in here. Unfastening the top two buttons of my long-sleeved shirt, I pull it over my head then slip into a tee and cargo shorts and grab my digital camera from its bag. I plan to shoot B-roll of the scenery and the local wildlife now to use for scene breaks and under credits.

Stopping at the window once more, I see Ashton's head is still on her arms, but the goat has chewed through the rope tying him to the fence.

"Damn goats," I laugh to myself as I gather my things and head out of my room and downstairs. I'm on a mission, and there's pep in my step.

I enter the kitchen and look at the bay window just in time to see the goat run straight into the waves. It looks like a small seagull might be taunting him, and the scene would be funny—if it weren't for the fact he's about to be swept out to sea.

Ashton's back is still turned, so she doesn't see the first wave hit him with enough force to knock him on his back. I don't know if this is a treasured family pet or what, but I know Ashton is upset, and the last thing she needs is another tragedy.

The beast falls over, his legs rigid and extended. He's rolling in the surf like a furry log, and I'm running at top speed out the back door and down the stairs. Mrs. C is on the back porch with her bird on her shoulder as she arranges paints near her easel.

I dash past her and she jerks back, holding the wall for support. "Slow your roll!" she calls out, but I don't stop to explain. I have a goat to save.

"Fucking teenagers!" the bird squawks loudly.

Ashton hasn't moved, but when she hears me shouting her name, her head pops up. "What's wrong?" she calls, rising to her feet.

I point to the ocean, where all I can see are four hooves sticking up like tree limbs in the surf.

"Goat's in the water!" I yell, but the wind takes most of my voice.

She doesn't seem to hear me, and she's frowning as I fly past. I only vaguely register her following me.

"Jean Claude!" she screams. "Oh. My. God. That stupid, damn animal!"

My shoes are off as I dive into the surf. There's not a minute to lose if I'm going to save him. The water is warm and salty, and thankfully I'm a strong swimmer. The surf is blasting in my face with each stroke. I grasp the rigid form, and I can't tell if he's dead or alive as I tug him under my arm and start for the shore.

He's frozen in some position of goat-fear. Still, I manage to keep his head above the water. I swim us both to safety, and once I can stand, I carry him like goat Cinderella to the shore.

Ashton waits at the edge for us, hands on her hips. "Is he alive or dead?"

I don't have a clue. *The damn thing must weigh fifty pounds.* I sink to my knees and lower him gently to the sand. Water drips off me as I lean into his face to check him out. He blinks slowly and lets out a long exhale. I guess he held his breath while he played dead?

"He's alive." I gasp, still winded from the swim.

"I don't know if I'm happy or sad." A grin flits across her face as she stares down at him.

I give him a little poke, and it seems to startle him into spryly jumping up as if nothing even happened. With a loud bleat, he gives us both a glare as he shakes like a dog then attempts to trot up the shore in the direction of the little hill leading to the house.

"Oh, no you don't!" Ashton runs after the mongrel, and I'm so exhausted all I can do is watch.

I'm just thankful I don't have to perform CPR on a fucking goat.

One thing's for sure, staying here is going to be an adventure.

Chapter 8

Ashton

Few things in life are as jaw-dropping amazing as Jax Roland emerging from the surf, muscles bulging, water running down the lines of his face, dripping from the ends of his hair... Jean Claude van Ram a rigid brown log in his arms, legs extended.

Okay, that last part I could've done without.

It takes less than a minute after he puts that asshole goat on the ground for JC to jump up and head straight for Granny's shrub roses. I don't even have time to say thank you before I'm charging up the hill after him.

"Oh, no you don't!"

My overwhelming sadness at the prospect of losing Granny's house, even my semi-gratitude toward Jax for averting Lulu's anger over letting her precious goat drown, are forgotten in the race to save my grandmother's roses. In addition to the house, they feel like my final connection to her, the plants she lovingly cultivated every year in her funny hat.

"Did you see that?" Mrs. C meets me at the gate. "He charged down there like Adonis heading into battle. It's been a while since I've felt so stimulated. Reminds me of the time Mr. C talked me into taking a bite of a serrano pepper."

I don't have time to correct her Greek mythology or even ask why Mr. C was always taunting her with hot peppers. "Where did that bastard go?"

She jumps back, confused. "Rufus? I put him in his cage. It was time for his nap."

"Jean Claude! He'll eat everything!" Pushing past her, I continue running around the house, weighing my concern about Lulu's anger versus killing that goat with my bare hands.

When I finally make it to the top of the hill, I see him, standing on the porch, his head plunged into the middle of my sweet olive, chomping away.

"Stop, you heartless bastard!" I catch him by the collar and drag him out of the deep-green leaves.

I look around, trying to decide what I'm going to do now. This jerk already chewed through the rope Lulu tied him with.

"Ashton." The deep voice pulls my attention to the top of the path.

Jax stands there looking all of sexy with his tee stretched over his broad chest and his wet hair pushed back from his face. In his hand is a silver hook and a thin cable.

"What is that?" I drag the goat to where Jax is standing.

"I had it in the trunk of my car. It's from a job I was doing. The owners had really big dogs."

"He can get out of anything. I told Lulu not to bring him here again."

"Lulu's your friend?" He comes to where I'm standing and clips the hook through a loop on JC's collar.

"Possibly ex-best friend."

"You can't really tether goats." He gently extends the silver cable into the yard. From the soaked back pocket of his shorts, he pulls a metal stake. I watch as he loops the other end around it and pushes it into the ground. "How long do you expect to babysit him?"

"She's got one hour left. Then we're digging a pit. Roasted goat is delicious."

The ripple of laughter from Jax's throat does funny things to my insides, and I try to remind myself I'm super pissed off... only, I'm not sure why. My head is so mixed up from last night to today to talking to Ben to feeling desperate about the future. I feel like I'm on an emotional rollercoaster, and I don't know what direction it's going to take me next.

"Listen, I'm really sorry." Shaking my head, I catch up with everything that just transpired. "You didn't have to run into the ocean and save him like that."

He presses his fingers to his eyes and huffs out a laugh. "I wish you'd said that earlier. Not that I'm the type to watch an animal drown..."

"Why did you save him?" Tilting my head to the side, I try to understand this sexy man who melted my panties one minute and squished my dreams the next. Who ran into the surf to save a dumb beast, and who could potentially be my knight in shining armor against my brother.

He shrugs, shaking his head. "I-I don't know. I guess I saw you sitting on the beach... I just thought you've lost so much. I didn't want you to lose any more."

"What makes you think I've lost something?" He looks like he's said too much, and I hold up a hand. "You know what? Just forget it. Lulu will appreciate you saving her ram."

"I hate to argue, but that guy is a goat."

"Yes, but Jean Claude van Goat isn't as catchy as Jean Claude van Ram."

Jax's expression is thoroughly confused, but his voice is gentle. "Either way, I didn't do it for Lulu. I did it for you."

I study him.

As much as I don't want to do it, I compare him to Kyle. My ex-fiancé acted like he cared about my feelings. He did things he said were for me, but I clearly recall walking into his dental office that evening only to find him getting drilled—and not by a dental tool.

Suctioned is more like it.

Whatever. The last thing I'm interested in is getting mixed up with another guy. The best thing to do is change the subject.

"Where do we stand on the rehab?" I ask.

He puts his hands on his hips, and his shoulders appear even broader. "I just got off the phone with my producer, and we should be able to cover everything with sponsorships."

My eyes grow wider, and I cover my mouth with both hands. "What are you saying?"

"We'll have to cut some corners, but not structurally. I won't use an assistant, so you'll have to be out front at times, following my directions." His eyes rove over me. "You're naturally photo-genic—and genuine—so I don't see a problem there."

I feel my cheeks getting pink. "Okay, but what? That means —"

"That means we're going to do everything on your list, and hopefully nothing pops up we haven't planned for." He pauses for a moment. "I had this crazy idea of redoing the sitting area, you know, since it's the first room everyone sees. With just a few, inexpensive touches—and maybe some furniture rehabbing on your part—we can give it more of a beachy feel."

"Really?" My voice goes high.

He nods. "I was thinking we'd paint the walls a soft white, maybe put in an updated lime green and blue rug. I actually get a big discount at Home Goods if I mention them on the show. I can get decor for almost nothing. As for the piano... Would you consider giving it a distressed finish? I mean, if you want." He shrugs and looks at me sheepishly. "Am I going too far? I tend to do that when I get something in my head."

Elation flies over me. I've been dying to update the entire house since the day I moved in six months ago. I jump forward, but I catch myself before I pull him into another unprofessional hug.

"It all sounds incredible!" I run in a small circle wringing my hands. Jean Claude bleats, and I glance over at him. For once he doesn't even annoy me—nothing does.

Take that, Ben!

Take that, Kyle!

Take that, everybody who said this was a fool's errand!

I'm going to restore this house, and I'm going to make it the most successful B&B on the coast. I'm going to show everybody. It's going to happen. I just know it. And this sexy guy is going to help me.

Chapter 9

I'm driving home from dinner at Bernice's, and I'm beat from my long day. At the same time, I'm strangely exhilarated the closer I get to The Conch Shell. I know I won't be able to sleep tonight, mostly because I can never sleep in a new room on the first night.

Hell, sometimes the first three nights.

I blame my restlessness on the fact when I was fifteen, and my mom sent me off to a boarding school in Connecticut where I was stuck in a cold as hell dorm with Upper East Side rich kids. It took me forever to acclimate. Rest assured, I figured out quick how to think on my feet and dish out as good as I got from those guys. It came pretty easy. I was already six foot two and fit from football and working with my dad.

I let out a sigh as I think of him. We lost Dad in a car accident, and when my mom remarried six months later, she decided I needed a more formal education to suit the Roland name. Figures. She always wanted to be fancier than we were, and as soon as she landed a rich husband, off to boarding school I went. Bernice went to a local private school, since she was a few years younger than me and easier to manage.

Admittedly, I acted out after my dad passed. I skipped

school, got shitty grades, and started fights—but it was just grief. Part of me has never forgiven Mom for yanking me out of my home. Whatever. I push that anger away and smile as I imagine what my dad would say about the antics we've gotten into on *The Right Stud*. Damn, he'd love it.

He'd love his grandkids too.

This afternoon, I checked in on Bernice and my triplet nieces: Molly, Mellany, and Mayla. Why the hell Bernice chose names that all start with the same letter is beyond me. Even though they aren't identical, I can barely keep them straight most of the time.

As soon as I came in, Mellany—or was it Molly?—jumped on me and demanded I be her pony. Three rambunctious pony rides later followed by an impersonation of a prince who wanted to marry the triplets, I was ready to pass out.

Thankfully, Mittens the kitten was safely inside, and I was treated to lots of grateful little girl hugs for that act of heroism. I told them all about rescuing Jean Claude van Ram as Bernice cooked my favorite meal, lasagna with French bread slathered with garlic and butter, and wouldn't you know it? Ashton's friend must be right. The girls decided Jean Claude must be a magnificent animal to have such a fancy name.

The lights are off when I reach the place, and as I make my way up the stairs to my room, my phone lights up with a text. I turn it over to see it's from the number I called earlier, the one Pearson sent to me about the beachfront property.

Thanks for the quick reply. If you're free, we can meet for coffee in the morning at the Java Hut. It's a small town. I'll know you when you arrive.

Frowning as I think, I decide getting this out of the way is a good idea. ***Sure. I'll be there at eight.***

THE RIGHT STUD

Once in my room I stand at the big window, thinking about my dad and watching the ocean curl into the shore. The water is black, and the moonlight touches the tips of the waves in silver. I think of Ashton doing her victory lap in the yard this afternoon. Her smile seemed to outshine the sun. I wonder how her evening went here without me, but just as fast I try to push thoughts of her away. I have a job here, and that's what I need to focus on. Business.

With a sigh, I decide to go for a walk to clear my head. It's too beautiful out there to ignore, and I can see why Ashton is enamored of this place.

Still wearing my jeans and tee from dinner, I grab my flip-flops and open the door. My plan is to be quiet and stealthy and it seems to be going smoothly, only it's dark in the hallway. The moon is shining through the oval window near the stairwell, and I use it to navigate.

Moving slowly toward the light, I've almost made it when I collide with someone coming from my left. Both of us exclaim with surprise, and I hear a soft groan. *Shit!* I definitely felt the crunch of someone's toes under my foot. I reach out to steady the weaving form, which is decidedly soft, silky, and female.

Goddamn, I hope I haven't somehow ended up in Mrs. C's room, only I quickly remember Ashton said she was downstairs.

The moonlight from the window helps my eyes to focus. "Sorry... Ashton?"

"It's me," she whispers. "I should apologize..."

I gaze down at her, my eyes now adjusted enough to see the outline of her oval face, the way her hair falls in thick waves around her shoulders. She's wearing a silky pink tank—I know because my hands are on her waist—and a pair of the shortest lace-trimmed booty shorts I've ever seen. *Is that what she sleeps in?* Her sweet, citrusy scent hits me, and I swallow.

Fuck. She's *hot.*

How the hell am I supposed to keep my hands off her?

Her small hands clutch my biceps. "I didn't even look up when I came out of my room."

"Late-night snack?" I'm whispering because the moment feels intimate.

"Actually, I was having a nightcap. If I'd known you were here, I might have taken more care." She pauses. "I didn't hear you come in. I guess I was in the shower." She looks down at her feet while I'm imagining her in the shower with a lemon-scented body wash…

"Are your toes okay?" I bend down to see if there's any damage from me stepping on her, but the light is shit. I look up at her. "I'm pretty handy with a smashed finger or toe if you want to come in my room and let me have a look?"

She blinks rapidly, her lashes fluttering against her cheeks.

Then I realize what I just said.

I stand up and laugh self-consciously as I rub the back of my neck. "I just invited you into my room…"

"My toe is fine. Don't worry."

I nod, wondering what the etiquette is for running into your hostess in her sexy silk pajamas. I clear my throat again. "I should have turned on the light, but I didn't want to wake anyone. It's just a new place makes me squirrelly the first few nights. Give me three days, and I'll be snoring like a bear. "

Her eyebrow arches. "Are you having trouble sleeping?"

"Yeah, I always do, no matter where I stay."

"They say warm milk helps you sleep. Want me to make you some?"

Laughing softly, I touch the side of her cheek. She's so damn sweet. "I think warm milk sounds… disgusting."

She exhales a breathy laugh. "I think you're right. Warm milk sounds pretty gross."

Standing here in the dark, quiet hall with just a few inches between us, I feel like even though we've made a little progress, I want to know her better.

"Why were you sad this afternoon?"

Lines form along the top of her eyebrows, and her eyes move away from mine. "I don't know what you mean. I wasn't sad this afternoon."

I do my best to make my voice gentle. "I saw you sitting on the beach, and your head was down. You seemed like the weight of the world was on your shoulders."

"The weight of the world." She repeats my words softly then sighs as she chews on her lip. "To be honest, since my grandmother died, I guess nothing feels right. She was the one person in my family who got me, you know? She taught me everything I know about cooking and gardening. We loved to watch old movies together—" A wistful expression flits across her face, but she stops. "I'm sorry. I'm sure you don't want to hear all this."

But I do. "You don't have any parents?"

"No, my parents are great, but they're retired and live in Boca, where their friends are, and my brother…" Her voice trails off.

"Yeah?"

She tilts her chin up, almost defensively. "Don't even get me started on him."

I nod. I can understand. My mom makes me crazy too. I'm thankful her society life keeps her busy enough that she barely contacts me.

Ashton continues. "Plus, I can't seem to stop picking men

who are complete douche canoes—" She comes to an abrupt halt, her lips tightening.

My ears perk up, and I remember Mrs. C mentioning a cheating fiancé. "What happened?"

Shaking her head, she turns away, almost as if she's heading back to her room. I can't let her do that. I like how she's opening up to me. I like *her*.

"Wait." I'm right beside her, gently touching her arm. "I'm not trying to overstep, but if we're going to be working together, I'd like to get to know you better. If you want to talk, you can trust me."

"Trust you?" Her eyebrows rise. "Trust you with what, Mr. Roland?"

"Jax." I grin, not fazed one iota by her bit of sass. "Call me Jax."

"Fine. Jax."

I smile. "So, what made you sad?"

She stares at the ground, her fingers plucking at the lace on her legs. "It's just my brother and family stuff. I can't really talk about it."

"Oh." I study her face, seeing the way she tugs at her lip with her teeth. Whatever is up with her brother, he's got her in knots.

"Anything else?" I ask. "What about this douche canoe? Want me to kick his ass? I used to box in boarding school."

She cocks her head. "You're rather nosey, aren't you?"

"Only about square footage."

Her lips twitch. "So why the questions?"

I grin. "The truth is, normally I wouldn't give a rat's ass about a girl's ex, but for some reason tonight... I do."

"Oh."

The temperature in the hall shoots up a couple of notches, and my eyes flicker to her mouth and up. Her eyes move to my lips, and I feel the weight of her gaze on them. She fucking wants me and I know it. We both want another dose of the insane chemistry we felt in that hallway at the Smoky Siren.

But she told you she isn't interested, my head says.

Fuck that.

"Ashton?"

She puts her hand lightly on my chest and steps forward, bringing us closer. "Don't worry about my war stories. It's enough that you're helping me with this job. You've made me happier than you could ever know." Rising onto her tiptoes, she presses her lips lightly against my cheek.

It's like an electric charge races through my torso and centers below my belt. Heat spreads, my cock rises, and I'm ready to grab her and hold her against the wall, find her tongue with mine and claim that mouth, claim so much more…

But just as fast, she's gone.

She steps away and whispers goodnight, leaving me standing in front of my door, frustrated as hell, and wondering what just happened.

Chapter 10

Jax

My alarm goes off at seven, and I'm out of bed. Shuffling to the bathroom, my eyes are still closed, and the scene that's been replaying in my head all night is back—Ashton in the hall, in my arms, in those lacy shorts, that silky pink top. Her soft lips against my scruffy cheek…

I shove my morning wood down and lean my head against the wall, forcing myself to focus. I wonder if she's awake yet, when I hear pots and pans clanging downstairs. Sounds like a yes, but I've got to head into Palmetto for that meeting at the Java Hut.

A notecard in a pewter tray on the dresser says a continental breakfast is served Monday through Friday from eight to ten with a full breakfast on the weekends. I should have just enough time to make it into town and back before anybody misses me.

After a quick hop in the shower, I emerge from my room wearing jeans and a navy polo. I step quietly into the hallway and dash down the stairs, successfully avoiding detection. I'm glad I left my car at the top of the driveway last night as I turn the wheel toward town.

Maybe it's my pride, but I don't want Ashton to know how much of a shoestring budget *The Right Stud* has. I don't want her to think I'm not legit or worry I won't be able to get her any new business with the exposure. It's not often I want to impress a girl —hell, I've never had to—but something about her is different.

Following the guide of my phone, I'm pulling into The Java Hut in less than ten minutes.

Sure enough, as soon as I walk through the door, a tall guy with cropped brown hair and a hard gaze stands and walks toward me, extending a hand. He's wearing an expensive-looking suit and flashes me a confident smile. I'm guessing he's either a lawyer or a salesman.

"Jax Roland?" he says as our hands clasp in a firm shake. "I got your voicemail about the property. Thanks for getting in touch with me so fast. Normally, I don't do business on Sunday, but I'm anxious to get the ball rolling on selling this house."

I nod and follow him to a small table with a dark linoleum surface. The entire place is retro, with murals painted on the cinder block walls, and a decidedly 1950s-diner feel.

"No problem." I pull out a silver metal chair and take a seat. "It made sense to do it now, since I'm in the area, Mr...?"

"Sorry, it's Ben. Ben Hall."

Wait...

"Coffee?" he asks as he waves to a waitress dressed in black jeans and a black tank. She obviously knows him and smiles.

What the hell?

Could he be related to Ashton?

"Uh, yeah, coffee sounds great." I nod as concern slowly washes over me.

He keeps talking. "I inherited the property last year, but it's been vacant until about three months ago. The main structure is in pretty bad shape. You'll probably find more value in the land than the house."

The waitress quickly puts a thick mug of hot coffee in front of me and hustles to the next table. Ben smiles as he takes a sip of his, and I see the resemblance. Still... I have to be sure.

"Where did you say the property is located again?" A lead weight is in my stomach as he recites the address for The Conch Shell.

"My sister's been there a while, sorting our grandmother's personal belongings. It's been a difficult time, but I think we're ready to move forward on this."

"Move forward," I say quietly. "On your family home. On the beach." I grimace.

I'm putting it all together. I remember yesterday when Ashton showed me to my room. She'd run downstairs to meet her brother, then I'd seen her just a short time later on the shore with her head in her hands. *The weight of the world on her shoulders...* It all makes sense now.

He lets out a sigh. "I don't mean to sound heartless, but the place is a true money pit. It's a wooden home, built in the 1940s directly on the beach. Nothing is to code. It's a maintenance nightmare. My grandmother worked on it all the time, but it's never been fully renovated."

It's like he's speaking my words back to me, and all I can see is Ashton's face, her sadness replaced with pure joy when I said I'd help her. I remember her spontaneous hug...

Now this.

"Of course, my sister and I have different ideas on the best way to handle the property—"

My brain ignites as his words, and I get an idea, a way to stall. "Wait—so you're not the sole owner of the property?"

He shifts in his chair. "No, but I'm the oldest. I'm also an attorney..."

I take a long sip of coffee. "None of that matters if you're a co-owner. Your sister will have to agree to sell, otherwise there's no point in even talking. You'll have to go through probate or buy her out. It's sticky and not something I'm interested in handling."

"You don't have to explain the law to me." He lifts his hand in a halting motion. "Trust me, my sister will come around. I just need you to visit the property and make us an offer. Once you see it, you'll understand what I'm saying, and once my sister sees your offer, her resistance will disappear. It's truly a gold mine just waiting to be tapped."

He's right. It was the first thing I'd thought when I'd walked around the place yesterday morning, before I'd rung that door-bell. Now my feelings have done a one-eighty. "Still, I'm not comfortable getting in the middle of a family dispute."

Ben Hall exhales and leans back in his chair. "I'm sorry to hear that. Blaine is a good friend, and I'd wanted to give him my business. I suppose someone else will have to help me with it…"

His voice trails off and I stiffen. My eyes squeeze shut for a moment, and my grip tightens around the warm mug. He's right. If I say no and walk away from this, he'll just go to the next guy on the list, and I'll have no control in the matter. At least if I work with him, I'll have some power over what happens. If it's me handling the turnover, perhaps I can buy us some time.

Leaning forward, I exhale deeply. "I guess if you put it that way, I'll take a look at it."

Ben's eyes lighten. "Great! I'm glad to hear it." He pulls out his phone and starts swiping. "I prefer working with people I know. I mean, yes, technically we've just met, but if Blaine sent you, I know you're the best."

It's true, I think ruefully. I'm the best all right.

My phone vibrates, and I pull it out, studying the familiar address for The Conch Shell he just texted to me.

"That's the location." Ben puts his phone in his breast pocket. "It's probably best if you go on your own and check it out. If I tell my sister we're coming, she's likely to come up with some nutty reason why we can't be there. If she sees us together, I wouldn't put it past her to pull some stunt."

"She sounds like a character." I know the truth of my words.

"You have no idea." There's exasperation in his tone that annoys me, but I keep my expression neutral.

We both stand, and Ben leaves cash on the table. "Just cruise by when you get a chance, scope it out, and let me know what you think. I'll be waiting to hear from you."

We shake hands, and I walk with lead feet back to my car. My heart is heavy in my chest as I drive to the beach. I pull my car all the way up the drive this time and leave it unlocked.

My mind is racing, and I'm sorting through what just happened and where it puts me. Ashton's brother wants to sell the place, but she wants to fix it up. It's why she invited me to come here.

Would fixing it up help her avoid selling it? I need to find out and see what I can do to help her. I'm jogging up the steps when I realize without the sale of this place, I don't have the extra money to invest in the show and in turn invest in the renovation. I guess that's what you call irony… or shitty luck.

"We'll just have to make it work," I mutter as I round the corner, almost flattening a parrot-toting Mrs. C coming out of her bedroom.

She's dressed in a bright orange kaftan with a pink turban on her head. "My, my, but you're always in a hurry, Studly. I hope you're not like that in the bedroom. Mr. C was as slow as molasses, but let me tell you, molasses is good to use in a pinch when you want to spice things up. Know what I mean?" She wiggles her eyebrows.

I don't want to know what she means. "I'm just headed to the kitchen for breakfast. Apologies for nearly running you down."

"Bacon!" the bird screeches.

She pets him on the head with her finger. "Now, don't be an asshole, Rufus. I won't let him eat it all." Her eyes go to mine. "Right, Studly?"

"I'm sure there's enough bacon to go around."

When we enter the kitchen, Rufus flies off her shoulder and perches on the tall curio in the corner, his beady eyes quickly surveying the place.

My eyes are eager for Ashton. I need to find out what's at stake for her in this renovation, and how I can help her, even if we're back to a shoestring budget—a shoestring budget with no cushion in case something goes wrong.

I can hear Tara's voice in my head. *Something always goes wrong.*

My stomach is tight, and I don't want to think about any-thing going wrong—especially not when I see sexy Ashton skipping around the kitchen. Her long hair is twisted in a messy bun on top of her head, and she's wearing that white apron. Her tan legs lead down to those cute little bare feet as she bustles around the kitchen. Damn, this is the way to start the day.

I watch her juggle some kind of breakfast casserole, and I grab a hot pad and take it from her as she removes it from the oven.

"It's a quiche," she says.

"It smells delicious."

"I hope so. I got up later than usual, and I'm behind schedule." I can see she's flustered as she tells Mrs. C good morning. Glancing at the clock, I see it's nine.

"I bet this guy can help you." Mrs. C points a long finger at me, and I have to check myself because she has no idea how much I really can help Ashton.

"I sure can," I say with a smile. "What do you need?"

Ashton tilts her head toward a black skillet. "Start the bacon —"

"Bacon!" Rufus squawks, making her jump.

She glares and flips him off. "Keep your feathers on!"

I smother a laugh. So this is how they do breakfast. Honestly, it's not so different from Bernice's house. I grab the bacon from the fridge and spread it out in the pan. The air fills with a sharp sizzling sound and the tangy scent of frying pork.

Ashton works next to me, her arm brushing mine as she reaches for coffee cups from the cupboard.

"Sorry," she says as she bumps me with her hip.

"No problem." My eyes travel over her face, lingering on her lips. I remember that chaste kiss last night, and how dirty I wanted it to be. How dirty I dreamed of being with her, everywhere I want to kiss her, all night long.

"The sexual tension is thick in this kitchen!" Mrs. C announces in her loud voice.

I start and Ashton jumps back from me.

"It is not!" She gives Mrs. C a side-eye. "We're just cooking."

"You sure are! It's getting hot in here..." She snaps her fingers and moves around the room singing. "So take off all your clothes."

Is she moonwalking? It's hard to tell under the kaftan. The doorbell rings before I can ask her how she knows a Nelly song.

"Cut up a jalapeño, and I'll get the door." She waves a hand over her head. "Just be sure to wash your hands good after."

"I am so sorry," Ashton says as soon as the old lady is gone. I notice her cheeks are bright pink. "I did not intend for you to be sexually harassed in the workplace. Mrs. C is nuts, but she's like family to me."

That makes me laugh. "You don't have to worry about me. I'm used to crazy." I think about my sister's house. "I like it."

She shakes her head. "Mrs. C is not usually so persistent. She seems to think I need a…" She finishes with a little cough. "I don't know."

"A good fuck?"

Her face goes from bright pink to red-hot, and she huffs out a laugh. "Who knows? Maybe I do."

I nearly pass out with how fast the blood rushes to my cock. My jeans grow tight across the fly as I imagine her spread out on the kitchen table naked, her tits in my hands as I lick her pussy for breakfast. Then, when she's screaming my name, I'll flip her over and take her hard from behind…

We're facing each other, and it's the Smoky Siren all over again. It's as if our dirty thoughts are telepathy for each other. Her lips part, and all it would take is one step and my mouth would be on hers. I'm ready to do it. My feet start to move, when —

"Who the hell are you?" An irritated male voice cuts in loudly from behind us.

"Studly!" screeches Rufus.

Some guy with ginger-colored hair and sharp green eyes is standing in the doorway with a scowl on his face. His eyes dart from me to Ashton, and I can tell he's measuring the distance between us.

"That, Dr. Kyle, is the man who's going to plow... right through this house and fix it. In more ways than one!" Mrs. C crosses her arms, looking regal.

I scowl right back at him, not liking his possessive attitude one bit.

"Kyle! What are you doing here?" Ashton's steps back quickly, the oven mitt forgotten as it slips from her hand.

Kyle? Is this her fucking ex? My hands tighten and my back goes ramrod straight. Judging by the way her fingers are trembling, whatever he did to Ashton was bad.

I'm ready to punch his lights out.

Chapter 11

Ashton

Isn't there some cosmic limit on the number of surprises one person can get in a month? Yesterday, Jax shows up in my kitchen, now Kyle? And what the hell right does he have to stand here looking all pissed off about Jax helping me make breakfast?

Granted we were practically chest to chest just now, and stepping back, I do detect the slightest bulge in the front of Jax's jeans. Lord, what I wouldn't give to see that bulge uncovered… or feel that bulge in all the right places.

"I didn't know you were open for business." Kyle's voice is formal, and he's eyes are solely on me, obviously doing his best not to acknowledge our guest.

"What's that supposed to mean?" My tone is sharp. If he's attempting some sort of double entendre, I'll whop him with a skillet and bury him out back, I swear to God. Like he has any right.

My ex-fiancé clears his throat. "Would it be possible for me to have a word with you? Alone?"

I stand listening to the sound of bacon sizzling and the coffee pot gurgling for the beat of ten seconds. Breakfast is mostly done, except for the muffins. Technically, I have time to chat. Still, he *is* an asshole.

My eyes rake over Kyle, the sting of his betrayal is still strong, yet I can't help but acknowledge that he's handsome in khakis and a sky blue golfing shirt—one I bought for him on our vacation to Maui last year. Today's Sunday, and I assume he's on his way to meet a buddy at the golf course. Ever pragmatic, he probably stopped here because it's on the way.

The tension in the room ramps up as Kyle and I stare at each other. I chew on my lip, recalling all the Sundays I stayed home while he golfed.

But then maybe he hadn't really been golfing? Maybe he spent those days with Monica. Familiar rage bubbles, and I don't even care that Jax is about to witness a show down with Kyle. I'm past it. Once someone cheats or lies to you, it makes you do and say crazy things.

My lips compress.

"Ashton?" His voice is more insistent now.

"I don't know," I say sharply. "What exactly do you want?"

His eyes flare slightly, and he has the nerve to seem annoyed. "I want to talk to you without all these people around."

Mrs. C is beside him, holding him in a grumpy glare. Jax is beside me, his fist clenched at his side, and even Rufus is overhead, looking ready to swoop down and do some damage. It bolsters my courage.

"Maybe I don't want to talk to you."

"For the love of..." Kyle pinches the bridge of his nose, condescending as always. "We were together for three years. You owe me at least a word, Ashton."

"I don't owe you anything. I trusted you." My voice trembles, and as God is my witness, I will not start crying. Swallowing the painful lump, I continue. "I gave you my trust, and you treated it like garbage."

Lowering his hand, he has the decency to appear pained. "It's true. I didn't value your trust the way I should have. Will you please give me just a few minutes of your time to talk about it?"

"Sounds like she already gave you your answer." Jax's voice is sharp as a knife as it cuts through the tension, powerful and threatening. "Time to go, buddy."

Kyle flashes steely eyes at him. "I don't know who the fuck you are, but you'd be smart to keep your nose out of places it doesn't belong."

The skillet slams against the range as Jax shoves it off the burner and steps to Kyle. "I'll put my nose wherever I damn well please."

"Oh, yeah?" Kyle steps forward as well, and I find myself sandwiched between what feels like two raging bulls ready to clash.

Jesus, take the wheel. If you're up there...anywhere...please help me...

Jax's face reddens as he glares at Kyle. A muscle pops in his cheek. "I suggest you get the hell out of this house—"

"This isn't your house, asshole!" is Kyle's growling reply.

"Okay, okay! I'll talk to you!" I cry, putting my palms flat on both their chests to push them back. Good lord, I can't afford the repairs if they really do start fighting in here.

"Why did you have to stop it?" Mrs. C huffs from the doorway. "Just when it was getting good."

Jax's blue eyes are blazing as I lead Kyle to the side door. He's annoyed I'm going with Kyle, but really it's none of his business. Sure, his defense of me is a bit thrilling, but he's a guy too, and I don't trust any of them anymore.

With Kyle following me, I steer him out to the back porch

and down the steps until we're standing several feet out of earshot. Still, I can see Jax and Mrs. C and Rufus are at the kitchen window watching us. Perfect.

Crossing my arms, I glance up at Kyle again, taking in the clean-cut jawline I used to love to press my lips against. My heart hitches, and I'm not sure I'm emotionally prepared to have a conversation with him.

We haven't really talked since I caught him with his dental assistant. He texted me a few times and even showed up at the door trying to explain, but I didn't let him in. There's a reason I don't want to see him: it still hurts.

He stares down at me, a flash of contrition on his face. "Look, I'm sorry about showing up unannounced but it's been so long. I thought we might finally talk—"

My scowl deepens. "It hasn't been long enough. Say whatever it is you came here to say and go."

He rubs his jaw and exhales deeply. "I have to confess, I didn't expect to see you this way."

I cock my head, wishing my eyes could spit literal fire at his crotch. "What way? Over you?"

"No." He shakes his head and looks down. "So pretty... moving on, not caring about me anymore. Who is that guy?" His eyes dart to the window, and Mrs. C flips him off.

I'm furious that he thinks he has the right to even question any man in my life. "Are you brain damaged? I was ready to marry you, Kyle. You threw our love away."

He bites his lip. "Babe. I got nervous. Or cold feet... I don't know."

"I can tell you what didn't get cold." My voice is sharp. "Your dick."

He winces. "I deserve that." He walks back and forth on the

sandy path behind the house. I don't move. "I think I made a mistake. Monica and me, well, she isn't like you and me. When I did that with her, it felt like…" His voice trails off.

"It felt like a hummer?" My voice drips with sarcasm. I can't believe he'd take my memory back to that heart-crushing day. "I'm not listening to this. Not another word."

I start for the house when Kyle calls after me. "She doesn't look at me the way you did. She doesn't make me breakfast. She's not my forever girl, Ashton."

I stop walking and look back at him. "That's too bad, because you ruined everything we had for a temp."

He's moving quickly toward me, closing the space between us. "I don't believe that. Let me make it up to you. Ashy, I want you back."

OMG. I want to die at the sound of his nickname for me.

"No."

"Just give me a chance." His voice is pleading. "You were so distant last year, and it made things weird. I felt so apart from you."

"My grandmother died!" Tears heat my eyes. "Can't you understand that?"

"Of course, I can, and I'm not blaming you. That came out wrong." He reaches for me, but I dodge his touch.

But part of me, a small part, wishes I could let him take me in his arms. I'd tell him about all my problems, about the business with Ben and how much it hurts. Instead, I push him away from me.

"I want to make it up to you," he pleads. "I was a complete and utter asshole. Will you let me make it up to you?"

My brow is furrowed, and I glare at him. How dare he plead his case this way, when I'm still vulnerable?

"Just think about it," he says softer, coming closer. "After everything we shared. Can't you give me a second chance?"

"I don't know." Shaking my head, I take another step away from him. "I mean no. I'm sorry for you, but I don't think I can do that."

"But maybe you can?"

I look up, meeting his eyes, and a headache is brewing behind mine.

"Remember the Christmas we spent here at this house with your Granny?" His voice is gentle, nostalgic. "Remember how much she liked me? We can have that again. I'll go to couple's therapy—"

"Stop. I-I can't do this, Kyle. You broke my heart, and now I'm alone. I have The Conch Shell, and I'm going to make it without you."

He lets out a deep exhale. "I refuse to accept that. You just need some time—"

"Ashton?" Jax appears on the path behind me, walking closer. "Breakfast is getting cold. We need to get going if we're going to conquer our list for today."

"We're still talking." Kyle's voice is stern, and the two men glare at each other, their rage barely contained.

"I need to go." My voice is quiet, and I turn toward Jax, ready to end this painful exchange.

"But you'll think about what I said?" Kyle says, trying one more time.

Without answering him, I pass Jax on the path and run up the steps into the house. I don't stop or even go to the kitchen. I continue up the stairs to the second floor, until I'm in my bedroom.

The first tear falls as I crawl into the large, walk-in closet where my grandmother's extra clothes used to hang. I remember weeping as I took them off the hangers and packed them up to give to Goodwill. They still smelled like her antique lavender perfume. This small space still has that faint, lingering odor of her warmth and comfort. So much love…

I sit with my back against the wall on the floor of the closet, resting my head in the corner. In front of me, hidden on the wall, is a large mural she painted of *The Little Mermaid*. It's the scene where Ariel is looking into a chest of forks, corkscrews, and assorted human paraphernalia. Closing my eyes, I brokenly hum… *Wouldn't you think I'm the girl who has everything?*

The door opens slowly, and I blink up to see tousled blond hair, warm blue eyes. Jax holds the door and looks down at me.

"Hey." His voice is soft.

Swallowing the thickness in my throat, I shove the backs of my hands roughly across my cheeks. "Hey."

He steps inside and drops to one knee before sitting with his back against the wall beside me, knees bent. A foot of space is between us, and he leans his head against the wall, looking up at Ariel.

"What's this?"

"My grandmother did it. For me. She was taking a painting class at the senior center. It's where she met Mrs. C."

He grins, his voice as quiet as mine. "Is that so?"

Nodding, I look at the mural. "I must've watched that movie a hundred times."

"She sounds like a really special lady."

My chest is tight, and I inhale, exhale, doing my best to breathe the pain away. "I was at this point in my life where I thought I had everything together. I thought nothing could ever go wrong. Then it all just started to fall apart. Like a sand castle when the waves come swirling in around it. It kept falling and falling. I tried to stop it, but it only fell faster, slipping through my fingers."

Jax is quiet, looking up at Ariel, his expression unreadable.

"God," I laugh, shoving my hands across my damp cheeks again. "You must be wondering what the hell you've gotten yourself into coming here."

"I'm not," he says, turning his head so our eyes can meet. The warmth in his smile soothes my aching chest.

"This place is all I have left. I can't lose it, too."

His expression is kind. "I'll do what I can to help you rebuild it."

"Thanks," I manage to say.

His warm hand covers mine, and he gives it a squeeze before lifting it to his lips. "I've been wanting to kiss you again since I saw you in the kitchen yesterday."

I snort a laugh, then cover my face with my free hand. "You're a true glutton for punishment... or you have a high tolerance for crazy."

"It's most likely the latter." When he looks at me again, a naughty gleam is in his eye. "Can I kiss you now?"

"You really want to?"

"More than you know." Leaning forward, he releases my hand and cups my cheek, but instead of mauling my mouth, he kisses my lips gently, softly. "I'm going to help you."

A genuine smile lifts my cheeks, and I believe him so much. Still... "Don't ever lie to me. Okay?"

His brows pull together and something flickers in his eyes. "I won't. I promise."

Chapter 12

Not telling Ashton I met her brother is not a lie.

I just want that on the record.

I had no idea the client I was going to meet was her brother, and I had no fucking clue he was going to ask me to give him an estimate on this house. The minute I realized, my brain went into problem-solving mode, trying to find a way to meet these two in the middle.

Yes, I could use the commission on a sale like this, but would I do it at the risk of hurting Ashton?

All these thoughts are going through my head as I hold the camera on her while she rips a rotten plank out of the porch floor. It's past four in the afternoon, and we've been working steadily on removing planks for several hours.

I keep the portable camera rolling as Ashton whips off her safety goggles and shakes out her long brown hair. She grins up at me, and I swallow. From her tan steel-toed boots that I insisted she wear to the smudge of dirt on her cheek, she looks like a construction guy's wet dream. "And that's how you tear out a board." She holds it above her head like it's some kind of championship wrestling belt, and I bite back a laugh. I don't know why everything she does is cute as hell, but it is.

I follow her as she stands up and tosses the plank into the dumpster I had delivered earlier. She turns back to me and puts her hands on her hips. "Shouldn't you be using a cameraman? Is he arriving later?"

Lowering the small digital camera, I look at it, thinking about my budget and the great shots I've gotten of Ashton working, of how necessity has been called the mother of invention.

"When I work alone, I use a cameraman, but in this case..." My eyes travel around the airy porch with its gorgeous view and even more gorgeous proprietor. "I wanted to try something a little more intimate and personal. I hope it yields something unique in the home-improvement market."

Her dimples pop as she smiles at me. "Well, hand it over. I want to film you. The show is called *The Right Stud*, after all."

She gives me a little eyebrow waggle, and I laugh as I hit the off button and let the camera rest at my side. I did spend most of the morning on her walking around the project and telling the viewers about the history of the house and how she inherited it.

She's in good spirits and part of me wonders if she's just pretending—but I hope she's pushed away thoughts of Kyle showing up earlier today. *Asshole.*

It was all I could do to keep my hands to myself when he demanded to know who I was and then dragged Ashton outside so they could "talk." If he ever comes back here...

I won't do anything, I remind myself.

She isn't my girlfriend.

Ashton isn't a girl I need to be messing around with. She's obviously still fragile from what asshole Kyle did and the loss of her Granny. I could hurt a girl like that. I'm not a commitment kind of guy, and I'd hate to lead her on.

She's come down from the porch and is walking to where I

stand in the yard. Her fingers brush mine as she reaches for the camera, and an electric current zips through my hand.

I push that feeling aside as I explain the camera to her, the on and off button and the zoom. She gets it right away as we stand there. She smells like summer with hints of fruit, and it's so hard to move away from…

"Hello?" she laughs. "Are you even listening to me?"

I blink and step toward the porch. "What?"

"I asked what scene you want to film and you just stared at me."

"Oh, right." I nod. "Let's do one of me explaining how to nail in the new planks. Ready?"

She nods, looking eager. "I'm actually excited about doing it. I mean, I took drama classes back in college and loved the stage, but I never imagined I'd be behind the camera. Any tips?"

I smile at her enthusiasm. "Just hold her steady and be natural. Comment on the work or whatever if you want. Have fun with it."

She nods and picks the camera up and focuses in on me as I get in position. "And rolling," she calls out and gives me a thumbs-up.

I adjust my Dallas Cowboys cap on my head and smile. "Hello, party people. The Right Stud is here with you on a hot summer day outside of Charleston, South Carolina, home to sweet tea and bless your heart." I toss out a cocky grin and give the audience a wave. "And don't forget those sassy southern girls. They are everywhere." I put a hand on my chest.

She drops the camera and laughs.

I stop. "What?"

She shakes her head. "Sweet tea? Bless your heart? You're one slick salesman."

I grin. "True that. I can sell anything. And trust me, the audience that watches my show is ninety-nine percent female." I strike a pose in my navy polo and show her my tightly roped bicep. "They love the way I talk, but most of all, they love to see me in action using these muscles."

She laughs, rolling her eyes. "You're so full of yourself."

I shrug. "If you're hot and you know it, why not use it? Now, let's get some footage."

Later, I'll go through it all and edit and splice it together. She gives me the thumbs-up again and the camera is rolling.

I tap my watch. "We're on hour three here at The Conch Shell and our hostess, the lovely Ashton Hall, is still at it. Let's hope this house can handle the both of us." I gesture to the porch and the pulled up planks. "We've been sweating hard and have gotten most of the wood pulled up today. Tomorrow will be all about installation."

I briefly go over the work we completed earlier in the day then turn back to face the camera. I'm about to point out the rotting crown molding on the ceiling when Ashton speaks.

"Tell us about yourself, Jax. How did you get into renovation?" Her voice is loud and clear from behind the camera.

She's still filming, but I play along. "Well, as most of you know, I'm originally from Charleston. My dad ran a construction company here called Roland Homes before he passed away. He started with nearly nothing and built a booming business. When I was little, he took me with him to work and let me hammer and play with drills. In fact, I still have the first tool set he ever gave me. He loved to work with his hands and…" Talking about him is never easy, and I'm not sure what to add next as a wave of memories washes over me. I change the subject. "And so do I. That's why I do this show. It's my mission to search out houses to restore." I wave my hand. "But you guys don't want to hear about me. Let's talk about this old house."

"I do," Ashton says. "Tell me about growing up in Charleston. What made you leave? I love this place."

I feel on the spot with emotion still pulling at me and I swallow, my brow wrinkling. Maybe it's the afternoon heat or maybe it's because I've been spending time with Bernice and the girls, but I feel a wave of homesickness like I never have before.

The camera light goes off and Ashton lowers it to her legs. "Jax? You okay?"

I rub the back of my neck. I don't know.

"Did I say something wrong?" She comes over to me, and I shake my head.

"No. I just... I don't know. Coming here. It's been a while since I've stayed so long. Usually I just drop in for a holiday gathering and check it off my list, but now, I'm actually staying here, talking about Dad... It brings a lot of stuff back."

Her eyes soften as she leads me over to a small table she and Mrs. C set up earlier with a water cooler and glasses. She pours me a cup and hands it over, gentleness in her gaze.

"What?" I ask.

She shrugs, the shift in her shoulder barely perceptible. "I know grief when I see it, Jax. I've been there. How long since you lost your dad?"

I stare at the ground before meeting her eyes. "I was fifteen when he was killed in a car wreck on his way to watch me play football. Changed my whole life."

Dismay crosses her face. "How terrible for you."

I inhale a deep breath. "He was my rock and came to every Friday night game no matter how hard he'd worked that week or how early his day started. He'd been working out of town on this big subdivision he was designing, and he was rushing home to see me play." I pause. "He was hit by a semi that crossed into his lane."

"I'm sorry." Her eyes drift over my face. "You were so young. Did you still have your mom?"

I huff out a laugh. "My mom is not an emotionally helpful person. I barely talk to her anymore. Apparently, I'm a disappointment to her."

She frowns. "How could that even be possible? Look at you!"

"She'd much prefer if I were a doctor or a lawyer, trust me." My mind drifts to the past. "After my dad died, I guess I acted out. I got kicked off the football team for fighting and ditching class. I came in drunk once and she flipped her lid." I chew on my lip. "She got remarried six months after he died, and I guess I went a little crazy and fell in with the wrong crowd. She shipped me off to a fancy boarding school."

Her lips part. "Oh my God. That's just normal teenager stuff."

I nod. "And all I wanted was to be home, but that feeling finally went away. I had to toughen up if I wanted to fit in."

Her frown deepens. "I'm angry for you."

I shrug, even though her outrage makes me feel better. "Don't be. I learned a long time ago that my mom is the kind of person who only gives you one chance. She's moved on and so have I." I feel uncomfortable, as if I've said too much, but I keep going. "She just doesn't care. It's not in her DNA or whatever. Some women aren't motherly." Mine certainly wasn't.

She shakes her head, clearly worried. "I'd never do that to a child." She stares up at the house. "Sorry, this is clearly none of my business, but I'm upset for you. I can't imagine not being able to come home."

I watch as she gazes at her home, and something in my chest aches. God, I want that. I want to look at a place and feel that kind of attachment.

I take my hat off and tap it against my leg, clearing my throat. "Sorry. I'm sure you don't want to hear all this personal family stuff."

She puts her hand on my arm, taking the cap from me, and puts it on her own head. "I want to hear everything about you, Studly."

It's the humor I need and my heart jumps at the soft smile she gives me. "Yeah?"

She nods.

"Everything?" I ask.

"Yep."

"Well, that hat you're wearing was my dad's. He was a huge Dallas Cowboys fan, and his dream was for me to play quarterback there some day." I grin. "A dad can dream, right?"

She takes off the cap. "Oh, I wouldn't have put it on if I had known…"

"No," I say, putting it back on her. "I like it on you. It looks better on you than me anyway."

"Tell me more about the real Jax Roland."

"On a dark and stormy night, I was born in Charleston, South Carolina. I weighed eight pounds, two ounces. I walked when I was barely nine months old, and my favorite food was sweet potatoes. On my first birthday—"

"Silly. Don't go back that far." She hooks her arm in mine, and before I realize it, we're walking down the cobbled pathway to the beach.

We sit on the sand and watch the tide come in and before

long I'm telling her about the triplets and how they'd giggled over Jean Claude van Ram. She tells me about Kyle and how she caught him cheating. Her eyes mist over as she explains the particulars, and I half-expect her to get emotional. She doesn't. Part of me wants to think it's because she's moving on…

I stop that line of thinking.

We move on to other topics and talk until the sun dips below the horizon. A soft orange haze settles over the water, and it's the best feeling in the world, sitting here with her. Seagulls race overhead, and periodically someone walks past us enjoying the beach, but neither of us seems to notice…

Chapter 13

Ashton

Kicking off our week of restorations, I set out freshly baked biscuits and homemade freezer strawberry jam I made with Granny more than a year ago. It's nostalgic, and it makes my eyes heat for a moment. At the same time, it makes me smile to have these little things she and I shared, these little pieces of her.

Normally I wouldn't take as much care cooking all my best, inherited recipes, but knowing Jax is going to sink his teeth into one of my flakey biscuits, well, it kinda makes me hot. I sniff and shake my head, reminding myself he is a man, and therefore he is not to be trusted. Still…

We sat on the beach last night until the sun had completely set and the night grew chilly, and we talked about, well, just about everything. The most amazing part of all? Jax Roland has a vulnerable side to him. I saw it in the way his shoulders slumped when he talked about his dad, but I also saw the joy in his eyes when he told me about his nieces.

I'm arranging the fruit and putting it with everything else on the buffet when I hear a mob of dogs barking outside. Lulu.

"Hello to the house!" she calls loudly. "Dang… Look at this. Wow!"

Sticking my head out the back door, I see she's left the five dogs tied at their special watering station, and she's walking around the porch with her mouth open looking all around.

The screen door slams behind me as I exit, following her gaze. "What do you think?"

"Did Jax do all this? It looks amazing."

The flood of optimism her words send through my stomach almost makes me need to sit. "It does look good, doesn't it? He really is a pro. I mean, of course he is. He has a show and all, but he knows things to look out for and little shortcuts. It would take me years to learn all this. If I ever did."

"I love the new trim work here." She points to the unpainted wooden cornices we installed late yesterday evening around the beams at the corners of the porch.

"The old ones were all rotten. I was able to pull them out myself, and you know I have no muscles."

Her green eyes go round. "He let you near power tools? Is he *insane*?"

"First, that's not fair. It was one time, and I'd never used a power drill before—"

"You'll drill your eye out—"

"I will not. I just took the paint off the edging." Shaking my head, I exhale an exasperated breath. "Anyway, I used a sledge-hammer." Then, I shake my head. "It was really just a crow bar, and Jax made me wear these giant plastic safety goggles."

"He really is a hero," she sighs. "I wish I'd been here to see him rushing in to rescue JC like that."

"You're lucky he was here."

She faces me with her arms crossed. "You say that, but you wouldn't have let my favorite pet drown."

"I wouldn't count on it."

We stand for a moment observing the fresh planks in the

porch floor, the fresh woodwork overhead. I imagine painting them in bright, happy colors as a salty breeze slides my hair off my shoulders. I can't stop smiling... until I feel my bestie's eyes on me.

"Have you banged him yet?" Her voice is conspiratorial.

My gaze narrows. "We have a professional working relationship."

"So have you banged him?"

"You are impossible." Dropping my arms, I glare at her. "I am not having sex with Jax Roland."

"Why the hell not? That is some Grade A, smoking hot manmeat if I've ever seen it. And he's a hero on top of it!"

"You said it right there. He's a man. I've written them off."

"What? You switched teams?"

"You know that's not how that works." My eyes narrow. "Anyway, Jax and I have to work together. We're not screwing it up by, well, by screwing."

"Damn, you've got some self-control. I'd be on that like white on rice. Like a duck on a June bug, like—"

"I get the point, and you're such a liar." We walk slowly toward the kitchen door. "You would never start a relationship with one of your pet owners."

"Have you seen my pet owners?" She levels her eyes on mine before shaking her fiery curls. "But who said anything about a relationship? I'm talking about a good old-fashioned roll in the hay. He has needs. You have needs. Scratch that itch, girl!"

My stomach is tight, and I confess, the idea of rolling around, wrapping my body around Jax's has me feeling flushed. *Grab the reins, Ash.*

"This is not a farm. We do not have hay." I reach for the

screen door and give it a yank. "Now, I just put out some biscuits and strawberry jam. Come eat."

The wind changes directions, and Lulu takes a step to follow me before seizing up and letting out a screech. "Oh, Jesus, save us! I'm going to vomit!"

"What now?" I turn to see her face is a mask of horror, and she's clutching her nose. Then it hits me, the smell of putrid, rotten eggs, or worse, something dead.

I grasp my own face, hissing. "What is that?"

"It's the skunks!" Mrs. C shouts at us, nearly making me jump a foot off the ground. "Help me close the windows, quick!"

I run inside, Lulu hot on my heels, and we frantically race around the downstairs, shoving the glass windows down as fast as humanly possible.

"Too late!" Lulu cries, still holding her face. "It's horrible! Make it stop!"

"I told you those critters were in the crawl space." Mrs. C is beside us, wrapped in a sea-green kimono robe with my oven mitt clutched over her face. "I was just about to take a shower when I caught the first whiff."

Dropping my hand, I try to be brave and not cover my nose, but holy shit. It smells like tires burning. "We do not have skunks!"

Rapid thudding comes from the stairs, and Jax appears in the room, a look of disgust on his face. "What the hell is that?"

I smile and hold my hands at my sides, even though my eyes are watering. "What the hell is what?"

His eyes widen. "Are you serious?"

"Cut the crap, Ashton!" Mrs. C barks at me before gripping Jax's arm. "Save us, Studly!"

Just then an ear-piercing yelp comes from the yard. It's

followed by more yelping, a cacophony of injured dogs.

"The dogs!" Lulu cries, snatching up a doily and running out the front door.

I'm right behind her with Jax behind me, and we're on the porch in time to see the poor collie, my favorite of the mob, furiously rolling on the ground and scrubbing her nose in the sparse grass.

"She must've gotten too close," Jax shouts. "You've got to take her home, bathe her in peroxide and baking soda. Or tomato juice. I've heard tomato juice works."

"It's okay… it's okay…" Lulu stands over the dog holds her hand above it without actually making contact. "Shit! I don't want to touch her!"

"Poor Lassie. Put her in your dipping tub!" I'm thinking fast. It's a good thing my friend is a dog groomer.

The little Chihuahua is shaking like a leaf, and Lulu scoops her up, grabbing all the leashes and taking off at a fast dash without even looking back. It's like DEFCON 1 around here, only instead of radiation poisoning, we're all trying to avoid skunk spray.

"Damn, Ashton." Jax turns to me, and I've given up. I'm clutching my face in both hands, eyes watering. "We've got to do something about this now. We can't work in this."

"But what can we do?" Thankfully the wind changes directions again, sweeping the foul, sulfurous scent away from us, out to sea.

I hear the noise of windows going up again. "It's like being trapped in a loaded outhouse," Mrs. C cries. "I'll set up some fans and put out bowls of vinegar."

"I've only read about this." Jax's brow furrows, and I can see he's strategizing, figuring out a solution.

I watched him do it all day yesterday while we were working, and it's kind of sexy the way the muscle in his jaw ticks as he thinks, the way he chews his full bottom lip... Lulu's roll in the hay suggestion flashes in my mind, and the space between my legs heats. You'd think the memory of that olfactory stink bomb would be a buzz-killer.

It isn't.

My eyes go to Jax's ass in those jeans as he walks around the porch, stopping to bend and look under it every few paces. "We need to try and find where they're hiding and block it off while they're out."

"I guess nobody's hungry for breakfast..." My dreams of Jax sinking his teeth into one of my buttery, flaky biscuits are effectively skunked.

Good lord, Ashton, focus. We have a real problem here.

He straightens in front of me. "Any chance you have chicken wire?"

"Come on." I lead him in the direction of the old garage. "I know we have some leftover lattice from when we planted the climbing roses." He helps me pull open the double doors, and we start rifling through leftover supplies leaning against the walls. "There could be some in the attic. Granny never kept chickens, but who knows what you might find."

He pulls the overhead door down and lowers the wooden ladder. It's wobbly, but once he steps on it, it locks in place.

"Just be careful. It's been at least a year since anyone climbed this thing."

He's standing with his torso through the ceiling, looking into the attic. "I think I found some!"

Half an hour later, after searching the ground for small holes —signs of skunks digging for grubs, Jax told me—we're climbing under the porch. I'm holding a light, and Jax has a small trowel in hand.

"It makes sense this is where they'd be," I grumble, doing my best not to get tangled in vines or put my hand in anything gross. "Nobody's on this side of the house."

We're in the far back corner, where the underbrush and sandy landscape creates a natural cave beneath the boards.

"Look what we have here. Hand me the light." I look up to see a small burrow about the size of his head surrounded by dark green leaves. The smell is stronger the closer we get. "I'll just flick this on here, and..."

For the space of one second, his whole body goes rigid, then he's backing out so fast, he almost kicks me in the face.

"Ouch! What's happening? What is it?" I'm sputtering and doing my best to crawl out of his way.

"Get out! Get out!" Jax grabs my arm and attempts to pull me with him. It only makes me face-plant in what I hope is just cold sand. "One's still in there!"

"One is—oh no!" A flood of foul-smelling odor fills the space around us, and I don't know how I manage it. I somehow get in front of Jax, escaping the tiny crawl space where we're trapped with the stinky thing.

The stench is stronger. It seems to be following me, and burning tears stream down my cheeks. "Run to the ocean! Take off your clothes and get in the water!"

Without thinking, I snatch the hem of my shirt and whip it over my head. I shove down my Pink capri sweatpants and leave them in the sand before charging straight into the waves and doing a dive.

Underwater, I hear the noise of Jax charging in behind me, and when I come up for air, I see he's coming up as well, grabbing handfuls of salt water and scrubbing them all over his... jaw droppingly naked body.

He's busy scrubbing his skin, but I'm drinking him in like water in the desert. As his hands move over his face and hair, his muscles flex, sending water tracing down every line in his round biceps, down the lines of his torso, down the V of his obliques, all the way to his long, thick cock, swaying heavy and tempting between his muscular thighs.

"Oh, shit." I feel lightheaded, frozen in place. My mouth is open, and I can't stop staring at him.

"Did it just get me? Are you okay?"

Blinking rapidly, I shake myself into focus. "What? You got sprayed?"

"I guess she didn't get me full on." He turns around, and fuck a duck, his ass is even better naked. *Of course it is!* It's tight and square, and it has those perfect indentions on each side. I want to bite that set of buns. "Otherwise, I think I'd really be burning."

Completing the circle, he stops and faces me again. The waves are still rolling in around us, but it's a relatively calm day at sea. His eyes darken as they drift down my heaving torso, and I realize I'm standing, soaking wet in only my thin, white nylon bra and panties... which are now wet and completely see-through. My nipples tighten under his gaze, and I shiver. Only, I'm not cold at all. I'm burning up and thinking about Lulu's advice about needs—living, breathing, red-blooded, healthy adult needs.

"Ashton..." Jax's voice disappears in the wind, but I quickly notice that long, thick member is as awake as I am.

In only a few steps, he closes the space between us, pulling me against his rock-hard abs. My arms go quickly around his neck as our mouths fuse together. His tongue finds mine, curling and stroking, and I feel a rise against my stomach.

I exhale a whimper, and everywhere our skin touches is fire. Our lips chase each other's. My arms tighten around his neck, and we break away with a gasp. He kisses a trail along my cheek to my ear. "I want to be inside you so bad right now."

It's like lightning in my veins. My hands move to the tops of his shoulders, and crazy thoughts drift through my head. I could shove my panties to the side and ride him like a stallion right here in the surf.

Right here in front of Mrs. C and everybody. "Dammit," I exhale, easing back. "It's too public... we can't do this here."

His expression is heated, and we're both breathing hard. We're both gazing into each other's eyes, and an inferno is blazing between us. It's like a grease fire, with the water only making it hotter, wilder.

As if waking from a dream, Jax releases me, taking my hand and leading me to the shore. He doesn't say a word as I watch him walk to his jeans and pick them up, holding them over his incredible cock before continuing to his shirt. He keeps going until he disappears up the path to the house, all the way inside, leaving me wet and needy and smoldering on the inside.

Chapter 14

Jax

It took every bit of willpower I possess in my body to walk away from wet Ashton in the ocean this morning. She stood there openly lusting after me, shivering and biting that full bottom lip in her transparent bra and panties. I could see her dark areolas, the sharp tips of her nipples... her bare pussy. She was any man's wet dream, and I still can't believe I was able to take my hands off her and leave. I've been frustrated and sick all day.

Fuck. Walking on the beach now, after dark, having spent the entire day as far from her as possible, fearing I'd lose my steely resolve, I allow myself to go back to that instant this morning when I knew I had to have her.

We didn't speak about it after I left her at the water's edge. I collected my reeking, discarded clothes and carried them to the garbage can, where I left them in a pile. Then I went straight into the house buck naked, thankful Mrs. C was nowhere in sight, although that bird of hers kept whistling and catcalling like it was a strip club. *How would he even know to do that?*

Never mind, I don't want the answer.

Once I was thoroughly scrubbed and sure the skunk was off, I went into town to buy paint and more supplies for our workday. I also picked up a heavy canvass tarp, coveralls, and a mask to use in relocating the skunks once they venture into the trap I plan to set for them under the house.

In hindsight, I'd overreacted. We most likely crawled through the spray they use to mark their territory, or the spray they'd ejected when startled by Lulu's dogs. If we'd been truly hit, our skin would have burned, our eyes would have been scalded, and we'd still be trying to get the stench off our bodies.

I considered all this as I took the long way back to The Conch Shell, as I stopped at a local burger joint for lunch. I drove along the beach road all the way up the coast, surveying property and drinking in the gorgeous views. It was late in the day before I finally returned to the house. Still, I didn't go inside. I parked near the old garage and crawled under the house alone to set the skunk trap in solitude.

My phone had been going off periodically the entire day, everything ranging from my sister calling to a few texts from Ashton's brother. I avoided them all, but not one was a call from her. I'm sure it's because she's thinking what I'm thinking.

The real reason I spent the entire day avoiding Ashton Hall is because that's not why I'm here. No matter how much I've craved her kiss since the night she branded my brain in the narrow hallway at the Smoky Siren, I have to remember who I am and what she needs.

She does not need a guy like me.

Ashton is beautiful and sweet. She's inquisitive and smart. She loves mermaids and nostalgia and this old house. She deserves a prince, a real hero, not me—the guy who's going to tell her brother he's likely right about this place. Ashton could never make as much money running it as a B&B as she could selling it outright. Not in a million years.

Without someone here to help her, the maintenance costs

will eat into her profits every year, and it will ultimately become a burden, weighing her down as she tries to find ways to stay on top of it all.

The truth of what I know I should say to Ben is a lead weight in my stomach. I didn't even want dinner tonight—I just came out here, walked up the shore a ways, and sat with my thoughts. I watched the sun set, remembering the night Ashton and I talked past twilight.

Now, with the moon huge and low over the ocean, I make my way slowly up the shoreline toward the house. The hush of the waves rolling in creates a calm soundtrack to the pale night. When I finally reach the path leading up the hill to the old place, I realize it was all a waste of time. Nothing has changed, and if anything my desire has grown stronger as the hours have passed.

At the top of the hill, the kitchen is lit up like a beacon in the night, and soft strains of Motown drift down to my ears. Ashton moves around the room, slow-dancing with a bowl in her arms. Her lips move, and I think she's singing along as she stirs. My stomach tightens as I watch her slowly sway in the yellow light. She's wearing a thin dress, and her dark hair is tied in a loose ponytail at the back of her neck. A few strands hang in pretty curls around her face.

Her eyes close as she puts the wooden spoon in her mouth, and I swallow the need in my throat. They blink open again, and she smiles as if she's thinking about something naughty. I can't take it.

My scalp is tight. The blood surges hot in my veins, burning under my skin as I charge up the path. I'm up the stairs, crossing the porch to the screen door leading into the kitchen. The door slams behind me, and she spins around, hazel eyes wide.

"Jax… Where did you go? I was just thinking—"

"I had to stay away. I thought I could distract myself, refocus…" I close the space between us in two steps and pull her soft body against mine. My hands grip her too hard, my voice is too rough. "I can't stop thinking about you, about how much I want you."

Her eyes darken, and she reaches out to put the bowl on the counter. "But we have to work together. It could cause problems…"

"Tell me to stop, and I will."

Every muscle in my body aches, waiting for her answer. Music floats in the air around us and everything is poised, waiting for what she's about to say.

Her pink lips part. Her tongue touches her bottom lip, and she says the words I've been dying to hear. "Don't stop."

Our mouths are together before she finishes speaking. Tongues unite, curling and caressing. She tastes like wine and sweet sugar. I pull her lips, nipping her with my teeth, devouring her. She moans, and it registers straight to my rigid cock.

Reaching down, I grasp her smooth thighs, dragging her skirt higher and tracing my fingers along the line of her panties, dipping inside to feel her slick and wet.

"Jax…" She gasps, and I lift her off her feet, carrying her to the stairs.

Her mouth is on my neck. I feel her taste me as she follows a trail of burning kisses up to my ear before pulling it between her lips. I groan deeply at the sensation. The heat in my pelvis, the pressure, is blanking my mind. I take the steps two at a time, crossing the landing and pushing through my door, kicking it closed.

She's on her feet, and our mouths are together again. We kiss like ravenous animals. Our hands are everywhere, fumbling with buttons, ripping at fabric. My jeans are long gone. Her soft breast is in my hand. *Did I tear her dress?*

She tugs at my shirt, and I step back, ripping it over my head. Then we're together again, her body so soft against mine, cool to my hot, delicate to my strong.

I kiss her shoulder, biting her skin as she makes those delicious little moans. She touches my stomach, tracing her hand down to my length. I groan, threading my fingers in the ends of her dark, silky hair to give it a slight pull. Her chin lifts, and I cover her mouth again, drinking her in, consuming her desire like a drug.

Lifting her again, she's on the bed, on her back, her hair spread all around. Her breasts rise and fall with her rapid breathing, and I jerk open the small drawer of my nightstand to grab a condom.

"You're so beautiful," I whisper, placing a knee beside her and lowering my face to kiss her flat stomach.

Her body trembles and she whispers my name. "Jax…" Her fingers thread in the sides of my hair. "It feels so good."

My lips move higher to close around a taut nipple as my hand goes lower, my finger tracing the line between her thighs before testing her wetness.

"You're so wet," I whisper, blowing on the hardened peak as I plunge a finger inside. Two fingers.

"Oh, God," she moans and breaks into a cascade of spasms.

Her arms rise to my shoulders, and she holds me, closing her eyes as she rolls into my side. I move her onto her back again, covering her body with mine.

"Did you come?" I ask softly before kissing the shell of her ear.

She does another little shiver, and I lean up to study her beautiful face. The full moon paints the world in black and white and silver. Still, I'm pretty sure I can see a blush on her cheeks.

"Kiss me," she whispers, and I gladly comply, pulling her full lips, teasing her soft tongue.

I give those lips one more tug before finding her eyes. "Do you still want this?" I'm hard and heavy between her thighs, dying for her to say yes.

Her knees rise, and her hands slide down my sides to my lower back. "Fill me," she purrs, and my forehead drops to her shoulder as I plunge into her.

The force of nature takes over, and we're rocking. She moans in my ear, and it's fuel to my fire. Placing my hand on the mattress, I arch my back to rise higher, go deeper. Her back arches, and I drop my head to kiss her breast, pulling her beaded nipple with my teeth.

Our loud moans and deep groans fill the air as I thrust harder, moving faster, chasing that fiery release. It's burning up my thighs, centering in my pelvis, until I break with a shout. I'm holding her body to mine, her legs wrapped around my waist as I pulse and fill the condom. We're on the tops of mountains. We're flying through space. We're a shower of starlight, illuminating the sky. *What the hell is going on in my head?*

I open my eyes, and we're both breathing fast. She's below me, and her eyes blink slowly, satisfied. Contentment unfurls in my belly, and I move to the side, gathering her in my arms.

My eyes are closing. These past few days, this morning, this night drift through my mind. "Why are you so sweet?" I'm not sure if I say it out loud, but I feel it so strongly.

From the tips of her pretty, bare feet to the ends of her silky hair, she's like a drug to me. She exhales a sigh, nestling closer into my side. She feels right being there, like she's always belonged. *What is she doing to me?*

Chapter 15

A steel chest is pressed to my nose when I blink awake, orienting myself. I inhale the dark and spicy scent of male and sex, and I cringe.

Fuck a duck. What have I done?

You boned the help, you hillbilly. You saw that tight ass in the ocean, and it was all you thought about all day.

Yes, yes. I can't deny it. Jax is definitely The Right Stud, because he just screwed my brains out in this big comfy bed... Twice?

I ease away from the warmth of his body with regret. The girl-power woman in me, rebelling at the thought of being duped by another man, has reared her mighty head and spoken: *I can't trust Jax Roland.*

Right?

But he made you feel so very delicious, my body reminds me as my limbs stretch out, trying to find the edge of the mattress as I slither away from his grasp.

The moon is high in the sky, casting an ethereal glow over his chiseled jawline and perfectly bitable lips. I did bite them at one passionate point. Yep.

Quickly, stealthily, I disentangle myself from his strong

arms and land on the floor with a plop. I freeze, hoping I didn't wake him, and I'm reassured when I hear a soft snore.

Thank God. I don't think I can face him right now. I made a complete fool of myself. It was the wine. It was the Marvin Gaye. It was...

Hell, it was just *him.* No man has the right to look that fucking good when he's washing skunk spray off his body in the ocean!

I snatch up my clothes and throw them on haphazardly. With one last, regretful look at his physically perfect form on full display, I open the door and slide out, closing it with a soft snick.

I've just made it downstairs in the dark, hoping to grab a glass of water, when I run smack into Mrs. C leaving the kitchen.

"Oh!" I stammer, stepping back.

"You got the big D didn't you?" A hint of a smirky grin is on her face, which is covered in some kind of green mask that smells faintly of cucumbers.

I don't even comment on it. "What's a D?"

"Don't play coy with me. I know a satisfied woman when I see one. I had that same look every time Mr. C took me to pound town." She sighs. "He had the biggest cock you know. I used to tease him that he could have been a porn star."

Pound town? Porn Star?

"You've been watching too much HBO, Mrs. C. Jax and I are in a working relationship, and I would never jeopardize that."

Her eyebrow arches. "Whatever you have to tell yourself, but your dress is on inside out."

"Fuck!" Rufus shouts from her shoulder, and I scowl at both of them.

"And don't think I didn't hear all the moaning and grunting. It was loud. LOUD. I kinda liked it to be honest. It's been a long time since anyone got a good seeing-to in this old house."

Pushing the hair away from my face, I exhale impatiently. "It's one in the morning. Shouldn't you be in bed?"

"I came in here to grind up some cucumbers for my mask. But I can tell you're not in the mood to talk, so I'll go to my room and wash it off." With an offended sniff, she turns to go.

"Wait."

She pivots back around. "Yes?"

I rub the back of my neck, which is sticky from being pressed against sweaty male-flesh for the past few hours of glorious bliss... which reminds me that I don't ever recall Kyle giving me two orgasms in one night.

Focus, Ashton. "If we *did* have sex, and that's a big if—"

"You did. I heard you cry out...*Oh God, I'm coming.*" Her face is deadpan.

"Did I make a mistake? I mean, he's here to work, and he's a man, which makes him an asshole." I give her a pleading look, and I know I must be desperate to be seeking dating advice from Mrs. C.

Her lips purse as she gives it a think, beady eyes carefully studying me from beneath the layers of the lime green mask. "Honey, he's the goat savior and the skunk hero. He deserves a good fuck. Just call it a one-off and let it go."

Unexpected disappointment hits me at the thought of it being just a one-time thing.

My ancient boarder isn't finished. "But if you're asking my opinion on Jax as a non-asshole, then yes, I think he's a good guy. What's wrong with having a little fun while he's here?"

I nibble at my lips, which are still swollen from his kisses. "I just don't want to get hurt again. I can't handle it. My heart is too full of... Kyle cheating on me."

"Kyle is a piece of dog shit. He's lower than a rattlesnake in a wagon rut, and he doesn't deserve your pain."

That may be true, but he fooled me. *Will Jax?*

She pats my arm. "I'm guessing you slipped out on him? Without even a thank you?"

I nod slowly, feeling an ache in my chest. I rub it. "Yeah."

She sighs, her expression hard to read behind the goo, but I see sadness in her eyes. "Bless your heart. Listen to me. Just go with the flow. Take what's offered with no expectations, and maybe, just maybe, he'll surprise you."

"Maybe." I head to the fridge and pull out a cold bottle of water and hold it against my face.

With a little wave, she and Rufus head off to bed, and I sit down at the kitchen table to think.

Give him a chance, my body says.

Run for the hills, my head insists.

What am I going to do?

I wake up at five, shower, and put on a flowy sundress. It's white with little daisies on it, and it makes me feel young and innocent —which is ironic considering the wanton hussy I'd been last night with Jax.

A whole-body blush warms me as I pass his door on the way downstairs. Pausing, my ears perk as I strain to hear if he's awake. I don't hear a peep.

Once downstairs, I quietly make coffee and set out some fresh fruit, croissants, and jam. My plan is to sneak out of here early and go for a walk on the beach, maybe stop off at Drifter's Coffee Shop to check out their latest confections and get some ideas for future breakfasts for The Conch. Even though Lulu isn't awake yet, I send her a text to see if I can stop by her place. I need to talk to her about what happened with Jax.

I'm stirring creamer into my coffee as quietly as I can when a warm body presses against my back. A nose trails up my neck, and warm lips kiss me, sucking gently on my tender skin. Sparks of heat fly all over my body, but I immediately stiffen, willing those tendrils of desire to stop.

"Mornin'." Jax's lips brush my skin as his teeth graze my neck. His voice is deep and husky, and I close my eyes and open them quickly, struggling, trying to gain some control. "You're up early," he continues.

My body trembles as his hands cup my shoulders and slowly turn me around. His blue eyes are sleepy and a dark scruffy shadow is on his chiseled jawline. It only accentuates how incredibly handsome he is.

He's not wearing a shirt, *dammit*, and his sculpted chest and six-pack abs are on full display. My fingers itch to trail down that body, slip into his pants, and see if he's hard.

He rubs his thumb across my lips, tugging my lower one down as he strokes me. "Can I just tell you how fucking disappointed I was to wake up and not see you in my bed?"

I swallow. "I-I had to think—"

Steely eyes study my face. "Regrets already?"

"Yes." My voice is a whisper.

Disappointment flickers in his eyes, but he quickly disguises it. "Why?"

He hasn't taken a step back, and we're so close. Our chests are inches apart, making it impossible to think clearly. I'm lost in a sea of desire and heat, but I want to be strong. *Why does he have to be the epitome of every wet dream I've ever had?*

His fingers push a strand of hair behind my ear. "Are you really going to deny the chemistry we have?"

"Yes."

He lifts a cocky eyebrow, clearly not intimidated by my proclamation. "Do I need to remind you how hot we were?"

My core lights up. The independent woman in me should be pissed that he's so arrogant and sure of himself, but even she knows the truth. Our chemistry is mind-boggling, and my body has no control.

"It was just a hook-up," I try to argue. "We got carried away by the wine and the music and…"

"Liar. You've wanted me since day one."

I inhale sharply. "I have not." Even I can hear how weak that argument is.

"I'm not an idiot. I know when there's something going on." His blue eyes drop to my lips, and his tongue slips out to wet his. My panties ignite. "It's something I've never had before, and I'm not going to let you turn it into a one-night stand."

My chest heaves. "Are you saying you want more from me?"

He cups my cheek as he steps closer. Our bodies are pressed together now, and I can feel his erection against my stomach. I know how long and hard and thick it is, how the veins line the velvety skin, begging for my mouth to suck—

He cuts off my thoughts. "I'm going to prove you wrong, Ashton. I'm not like your ex. I'm not him."

God. *His words.* He's saying all the right things. "How?"

He leans in closer. "Spend the day with me."

"And do what?"

"Fuck?"

I huff out a little laugh. I like his brutal honesty, and the images it conjures up. "We have work to do."

His eyes rake over me, lingering on the deep plunge of my dress. "I can work on you."

My legs are jelly. "Right."

He curls a hand around my waist and slips it down to cup my ass. "Is Mrs. C awake?"

I shake my head. The power of speech deserted me at his firm touch.

"Good. Let's begin."

He kisses me long and hard and deep, his tongue curling and tangling with mine. I hold on to keep from collapsing. His mouth lights a fire I don't know if I'll be able to put out. I don't want to put it out. I'm pressed against the kitchen counter and our lips are ravenous, chasing and clinging. He smells so good, spicy and warm from his bed.

"I can't get enough of you," he murmurs as his hand moves down to lift the hem of my skirt. Within seconds, his fingers have slipped inside my panties, and he's teasing my clit with delicate brushes before slipping two fingers into my core.

"Jax…" My pussy clenches around him, and I'm riding his hand, trying to get him right where I want him. It's as if he knows and deliberately avoids that one sweet place.

"Spread your legs for me." His voice is commanding, and I can't obey fast enough, parting my thighs until his access is unfettered. "Now lean back."

I'm panting as I arch my back against the counter and he kisses down my throat, nipping at my skin as his fingers dance across my clit, strumming lightly.

"Yes," I moan.

"You want more?"

I nod, and he goes to his knees, ripping my panties to a piece of lavender fabric in his hands. I look down, and he's looking up at my body. His burning gaze flickers to mine. "You're the most beautiful woman I've ever seen. I want to eat you. It's all I've thought about from the moment I woke up and you weren't there. I need another taste."

Even though we're in the kitchen in the bright glow of the morning sun, I bask in his words, feeling confident and more alive than I ever have as a woman. Jax Roland wants me desperately. He thinks I'm beautiful. It's enough to send me over the edge.

"What are you going to do about it?" I'm in now. I need the release. I fucking need *him*.

He gives me a slow smile, eyes heavy with lust. "I'm going to make you come in sixty seconds."

"Impossible." My words are garbled as his fingers move rapidly over my bud.

"Challenge accepted."

My legs spread wider. "Prove it," I say, feeling more brazen than I ever have.

"Pull up that dress and hold on." His gaze is electric as he watches me follow his orders.

I clutch my hem as his head dips down and his tongue licks my pussy in one long intoxicating swoop, twirling around my clit. My moans fill the air around us. Over and over he takes me, sucking and flicking, his fingertips sending waves of ecstasy through me. He devours me as if I'm his last meal. He's enthusiastic and loud, and I feel like I might collapse.

Sensation, warm and wonderful, gathers in my body. My spine tingles and I'm about to combust.

"I fucking love this," he says, the scruff on his jaw brushing over my core as his finger slides inside, curling around my G-spot.

I tense and writhe and hold a hand over my mouth to quiet my involuntary noises. I'm rocking my hips, my body undulating against his face as I come. Several seconds pass as the reverberations of my orgasm slowly fade. Gasping his name, I pull his head up to stare into his eyes.

Standing, he wipes the back of his hand over his mouth, those magnetic eyes still holding mine, taking in my face, which I know is flushed bright red from exertion. Hair sticks to the sheen of sweat on my skin, and my dress falls from my hands, covering my quivering legs.

How is it possible he's still dressed? He grins at me and flashes my panties. "I'm keeping these for payment. Don't ever leave my bed again without telling me goodbye. Got it?"

I bite my lip. Damn, I like him all bossy.

Our chests heave as we stare at each other, and the moment feels important. It feels momentous. I gave in to him. I think I want to do it again. Soon. Maybe in the next five minutes. I eye the kitchen table and imagine him behind me, his long cock sinking into me, hard and fast. *Shit*.

Mrs. C waltzes into the room, and Jax and I both jerk to a halt. She's humming, "She'll be coming around the mountain when she comes…" and my eyes are huge. Jax gives her a quick look before stuffing my underwear into his pajamas pants.

Mrs. C comes to a halt when she reaches us, her eyes bouncing from me to Jax. "Are you two going to move so I can get some coffee or what?"

I clear my throat and step to the side, grabbing a croissant and holding it out to Jax. "Here you go, all warm and toasty just like you asked. Don't forget the jam!"

My voice is unnaturally high, but damn if I can help it. He takes it from me, a bemused expression on his face. He doesn't look embarrassed one bit.

"…when she comes…" Mrs. C sings as she pours creamer in her coffee.

Good lord. Did she hear us? *Again?* Mortification flies over me. I hope not. Because what we did sure as hell had to be a health code violation, and if I'm serious about running a B&B, I have to stop having orgasms in the kitchen.

I clear my throat. "If you'll excuse me, I need to head upstairs for a bit." *And put on some underwear.*

Jax grins. "Me too. Guess I need to get dressed if we're going to paint the porch today." He runs his eyes over me lazily, a gleam there. "You might want to put your work clothes on."

I give him a quick nod and dash up the stairs ahead of him. Am I doing the right thing here? Am I really going to give him a chance? God, I don't know what I'm doing.

Chapter 16

Jax

"Need more paint?" Ashton's pretty hazel eyes blink up at me, and I glance over my shoulder, taking in the white tank top and tight denim shorts she's wearing.

Her brown hair is up in a messy bun, as usual, and my lips curl in a grin as I think back to last night when I'd wrapped that hair around my fist, pulling it, making her call my name—more than once.

We were fucking incredible together in the sack. I've known we would be from the moment I saw her at that stupid bar, from the moment our lips met and undeniable attraction blazed between us. Something about her pricks at me, digs under my skin. She brings alive every fucking molecule in my body, and it's all I can do not to pull her close and plant a kiss on her full lips right now.

I'm also not an idiot. Or maybe I am. Fuck, I don't know what I'm doing encouraging this thing between us. I just know I can't resist her, and I can't see any harm in following this through to the end.

I think back to when I'd woken up this morning and realized she'd left me. *Me.* She'd snuck out of my room without even a howdy-do—something that has never fucking happened to me before. Usually, I'm the one saying goodbye. Hell, at least I *say* goodbye. She didn't say a word.

Disappointment, irritation, and possibly desire, drove me down the hall to her room, where she was not. I threw on a pair of flannel pajama pants and made my way downstairs, and the rest is history. I wanted to be angry with her, but when I saw her, all the bad feelings flew out the window.

I watched her making coffee, a worried expression on her face, and I knew *I* was the reason for her worry. Something shifted inside me—something weird and strange and completely new. I wanted to prove to her that I'm not like her ex. I'm not a cheating, lying asshole.

She's still waiting, her brow crinkling in a frown. "Jax?"

"Sure," I say, taking a few steps down from the stepladder and walking over to her. "Give me some more paint."

The camera is off, and she places it on the worktable. We're taking turns filming as we paint the new boards and crown molding around the floor, ceiling, and corners of the porch. We've been working since around eight this morning, and we've gotten excellent footage.

I think about the morning sun casting Ashton's curves in glowing light. I think about the curl of her dark hair falling lightly onto her cheek, the way she pulls a pouty lip beneath her teeth as she paints, and I grin. It's possible some of my video of her is on the more "artistic" side of the home renovation spectrum.

In other news, we took a break to help Mrs. C get her paints and easel set up on the beach. We'd also managed to get a humane animal control company to come and help us with the now-full trap I'd set yesterday evening for the skunks. Those stinky squatters have been successfully relocated, hopefully somewhere far, far away. In any event, the chicken wire is in place around the problem areas beneath porch, and I don't see critters being an issue again any time soon.

Still, if I think about it, wasn't it the skunks that brought us together? Damn. Who would have thought that a brush with stink would lead to us screwing around?

"What are you grinning at?" Ashton says as I approach her.

I didn't even realize I was smiling. "You about ready for lunch? I could really use some alone time with you."

There. I said it. I want her again. My cock is already hard.

Her eyes dart from me to the house to the beach where Mrs. C is. "Uh, maybe we should go out?"

I nod and lean closer. "Afraid to be alone with me in the house?"

"Of course not." She swallows, such a terrible liar. "I just thought you… and I… might like a change of scenery."

I glance down at my clothes. There's not much paint there because my painting skills are sharp as hell, but it's enough. "Sure. Let me change, and we can go."

"Fine." She clears her throat. "Want to meet me in say twenty minutes?"

"You're welcome to come upstairs with me if you want." My hand curls around her neck, and before she can protest, I press my lips lightly against hers.

She inhales and freezes for a moment before her mouth melts into mine. Then we're kissing harder, longer, our breaths mingling together, hands grasping.

Pulling back, I stare down at her. "I've been wanting to do that since this morning."

She blushes. "Me too."

Heat zips through me. "I'm serious. Let's go to my room. Or

yours. I can't get enough of you, Ash."

Her eyelashes flutter. "I like it when you call me Ash."

"Yeah?" I've backed her into a corner of the porch away from the prying eyes of Mrs. C. "I can call you that while I fuck you. Something like, *Yes, Ash. God, yes, Ash...*"

"Fucking teenagers! Fucking!" comes from the open window as Rufus glares at us.

We both startle and then laugh. I glare daggers at the red and blue macaw as Ashton pulls away from me. "That bird is a real buzz-kill."

She smiles. "Let's do lunch in town. It's been a while since I've gone to certain places because of all the gossip. Maybe it's time I showed them I'm doing just fine."

Her cute chin lifts defiantly, and a fierce, protective pride warms my stomach. You bet I'll help her show those assholes she's doing fine. She's doing more than fine.

I tip my ball cap at her. "It's a date."

Chapter 17

Ashton

Jax wheels his shiny gray Audi S8 up to the curb, and it comes to a stop.

"Don't move." He gives me a wink before hopping out, and I squeeze my thighs together, watching the way his dark jeans hug his tight end as he closes the door and rounds the front to help me out.

"Such a gentleman." I grin, taking his hand.

I pulled on a short red wrap dress with tiny white polka dots and a cute ruffle around the hem before we left the house. The neckline is a plunging V, and the way Jax's eyes darken as they trace the swell of my breasts makes my entire body heat right up. I'm also wearing slip-on wedges so my red toenails peek out. I can't forget all the things he said yesterday, including loving my bare feet.

"Where too?" He pulls my hand into the crook of his arm, right next to his round bicep peeking out from the tight short sleeve of his forest green polo shirt.

"It's been a while since I've been to the Silver Spoon." It's a cute little high-end bistro for ladies who lunch and their boyfriends (or husbands, I guess).

We stroll up to the bright yellow cottage with boxes of

wildflowers along the white fence and at the windows. My chest squeezes in nervous anticipation. I expect at least a few of Palmetto's biggest gossip hounds to be present.

"Welcome to the Silver Spoon. Just two today?" The perky blonde hostess picks up two menus as I nod. "Right this way."

The white-covered wooden tables are close together in this converted old house, and with a stab of shame, I see one group includes the mouth of the south herself, Rayleen Jennings and my nemesis, Monica with the good veneers.

I hold my head high as we pass the table of four women, but of course, the hostess stops at the small two-seater right beside them. "Your waiter will be right with you."

I'm momentarily paralyzed, but Jax's warm hand touching my lower back as he holds my chair helps me get myself together. Thankfully, he's facing their table, and I'm pleased with the way he keeps looking at me like I'm going to be the main course again. Still, I can't lean into it. Even though Jax is ten times the lover Kyle ever was and twice as handsome, residual shame and embarrassment hold my stomach in a tight fist. I'm sure I won't be able to eat a thing.

"Hello there, I'm Oliver. Can I start you out with drinks?" A young man in a long-sleeved polo with a white apron around his waist smiles expectantly.

"I'll have a glass of prosecco." I want to ask for a double shot of Grey Goose, but I'm afraid that will give me away.

"Whitehouse IPA for me," Jax says.

My hands are in my lap, and I notice they're twisted together. I force them to relax as Jax's phone buzzes. He lifts it, and the smallest frown tweaks his eyebrows before he silences it and returns it facedown to the table. Our eyes meet, and he grins, leaning back for the waiter to place our drinks in front of us.

I want to ask if everything's okay, but he lifts his glass. "To progress."

"Progress." I clink his glass and take a long sip of sparkling wine, hoping it'll kick in fast.

Behind me the low murmur of female voices grows slightly louder, and I hear Rayleen's rise above the rest. "I suppose that's one way to meet a man. Open your house up to *boarders*."

The implication in her tone makes my blood race, and I take another, longer sip before returning my now almost empty flute to the table.

Jax's blue eyes are on me, and my nose wrinkles when I hear Monica's breathy reply. "What would her grandmother say?"

My teeth clench, and I'd love to tell that bimbo exactly what my grandmother would say to her cheating, fiancé-stealing ass.

Jax leans closer, studying my face and no longer smiling. "Do you know those women?"

Blinking rapidly, I force a smile as our eyes meet. "Only for about fifteen years."

Oliver cuts in before I can elaborate. "Have we decided what we want?" His voice is perky, and he holds a small black book. "Our special of the day is the old-fashioned chicken salad with grapes and pecans. It is *delish*."

"I'll take that," I say quietly.

He grins, waving his hand, and his cheerfulness eases the tension growing in my chest. "I'll have that right out for you. And another prosecco?"

I smile up at him. "Yes, please."

"And for you sir?"

Jax is frowning at his menu. "Got anything for a man on here?"

Our waiter's eyes dazzle. "A man, you say? How about a

good pork… tenderloin?"

I snort, finishing off my sparkling, and Jax narrows his eyes at me. He grins up at Oliver. "Sure, bring me the pork tenderloin sandwich."

"You got it, big guy." He takes our menus and folds them together. "Don't worry, mama, I'll have that fresh prosec right out with your salad."

A wink and he's gone, and I feel like my rear shield has left me… which is funny. I start to laugh again, and I realize I might need to slow down on the wine.

Jax leans back in his chair, his blue eyes sliding over my body. "I'm still sorry we didn't stay at The Conch for lunch."

"And miss out on the pork?" I can't resist teasing him.

"You wouldn't have missed out." His cocky grin makes me cross my legs.

Leaning forward, I drop my voice. "You would have given me some pork?"

He laughs, and the low vibration does funny things to my stomach. "A full seven inches."

My core clenches at the memory. "Bad boy."

"You know it." His eyebrows arch over sparkling, sexy blue eyes.

I feel all warm and buzzy. I want him to laugh. I want to show those jealous bitches behind me how much fun I'm having with my *male boarder*.

"So you didn't answer my question about those women—"

Oliver is back, holding my fresh glass of wine and directing a shorter guy carrying a large, black tray. "Chicken salad here. Pork for the man." I swallow a laugh, and he places my glass in front of me. "Here you go, my dear, and can I bring you two anything else?"

"We're good." Jax gives him a pretend-annoyed glance.

"All right then. Enjoy!"

He's gone, and I take a small bite of the salad. Huge chunks of white chicken breast are mixed with what looks like light mayo, pecans, and large purple grapes cut in halves. It's an explosion of tangy, sweet, and smoky in my mouth, and I let out a little moan.

Jax's gaze burns into mine when I open my eyes again. "Keep making sounds like that, and I'll have to take you to the car."

My stomach flips, and I feel a flush climbing my neck. "Promises, promises."

I don't know where this sassy sex kitten is coming from, but I'm going with it. I'm sitting here in a red dress drinking sparkling wine with the hottest guy ever to hit this town, and Monica and Rayleen can suck it.

My moment of preening is cut short when I hear Rayleen's quip. "At least *you* know how to keep a man, Mon."

Monica huffs, and I hear the shuffle of chairs. "I heard she'll be lucky if she even keeps her house."

Heat filters into my vision, and I reach for the flute in front of me, noticing my hand tremble as I bring it to my lips. Jax pauses mid-bite and lowers his fork. His eyes flicker to the women I feel standing behind me, and he clears his throat, rising to his feet.

"What are you doing?" My voice is a hushed whisper, and my eyes go huge.

"Excuse me." He steps from around the table, and I literally cannot breathe. "Do I know you?"

"Me?" Monica's breathy voice goes high, and I shift in my chair to see her. "I don't think so. I'd remember meeting *you*."

She steps closer, batting her lashes and cocking a hip to the side. She's actually flirting with my lunch date right in front of me. I'm ready to stand up and toss my drink in her face, but Jax isn't finished.

"You're right." He shakes his head and gives me a wink. "You only look like a manipulative, two-timing sneak I know. I heard she ended up a lonely old hag. They found her body... eaten by her own cats."

"Oh my goodness!" Monica's stupid head jerks back, and she clutches her chest.

"Karma's a bitch." He shakes his head, returning to his seat and reaching across for my hand. "You never have to worry about that, Ash. You're honest and genuinely sexy. Only good things will come to you. Unlike some people."

I'm doing my best not to laugh at his ridiculous story. Monica makes some huffy noise, and she, Rayleen, and their friends prance to the front of the café.

Oliver appears out of nowhere and slides the check onto the end of our table. "Bravo," he chuckles. "You can pay that up front when you're ready, Mr. Man."

We're alone, but Jax is still holding my hand, sliding his thumb over the backs of my fingers. Our eyes meet, and my smile is pure gratitude.

"Thank you."

His lips curl into a smile. "No thanks necessary. I wasn't about to sit here and let them talk about you that way."

Shaking my head, I pull my hand out of his. "You don't have to feel like you need to defend me—"

His phone rings on the table, and he scoops it up. Again, I notice a ghost of a frown pass over his features, and again, he silences it and puts it facedown on the table. I can't help being incredibly curious as to who keeps calling and texting him—who he keeps ignoring.

Tilting my head, I nod. "You can take that if it's important."

"It's just the office." He lifts his glass, finishing his beer.

"About the show?"

"No, it's my other office. I also do real estate work."

"Real estate? Like selling houses? You're a Realtor?"

His brow lowers, and he slides a finger down the side of his now-empty glass not meeting my eyes. "Not exactly."

He shifts in his chair, seeming uncomfortable, and suspicion like muscle memory flashes in my chest. I've had experience with men dodging easy questions, and the last time it ended with me looking like a fool.

Like when I'd planned for Kyle and me to visit the over-priced caterer, and he'd claimed to have a weekend business trip. I later found out he'd spent the weekend *porking* Monica.

"It's not a hard question, Jax. Either you are or you aren't." My tone is icy, and his eyes fly to mine.

I'm sure he sees my walls ready to shoot back into place.

"You're right." He exhales, relaxing his expression and giving me an easy smile. "I'm not a Realtor. I acquire property for a real estate developer. I guess I should have told you from the start, but I didn't want you to think I wasn't committed to our renovation project. I'm actually cutting down to part-time on the real estate end, hoping to go full-time on the show. But it hasn't happened yet, so they still call me from time to time with work."

I think about this for a few seconds, turning it over in my mind. "What's the name of the developer?"

"Pearson Real Estate. I've been with them several years."

"And you're turning down work... because of me?"

He hesitates over his reply. "Not exactly."

"But you're not taking their calls." I'm not sure how I feel about this new information. Is it because of me or is it because of his show? Do I want to know the answer to that question?

"It's not where my heart is." His eyes rise to mine again, and that look is back—the one he gave me this morning in the kitchen. The one that makes my insides feel hot and cold and flustered and eager all at the same time.

It's not a look I want to see from him—or any man—right now, and I scramble for a distraction. "Okay, well, I really think we should check in on Lulu. I sent her a few texts, but I need to go by and be sure she and the dogs are okay, especially Lassie. I love Lassie."

I'm talking a mile a minute, and I'm out of my chair, pushing it under the table and moving toward the door. Jax quickly scans the check and puts several bills on the table.

"Oh!" I start back toward him, lifting my bag. "I'm sorry—how much do I owe?"

His lips press into a frown. "Are you kidding me?"

"Not at all." My wallet is open in my hand, but he covers it with his two larger ones.

"My treat."

"But you wanted to stay at the house—"

"Do we need to drive to Lulu's?" He takes my arm, guiding me toward the front of the small restaurant. "It's really a nice day for a walk."

My shoulders drop, and I close my wallet, slipping it into my purse before taking his arm. "It's just a few blocks away. We can walk pretty easily."

Outside, the sun is shining, and my moment of panicked suspicion has passed. I think about stupid Monica and Rayleen and their minions, and I think about how Jax stood up for me.

My chest warms, and I'm not sure why I'm fighting the possibility of Jax having feelings for me. Mrs. C has faith in him, and here he is, essentially confessing he's turning down other work to help me.

My hand is in his, and he gives me a smile. I glance up at the sun shining through his hair, the kindness in his eyes. Could he be the white knight I've been waiting for after all?

Chapter 18

Jax

Ben is calling. Blaine is calling. I'm ignoring all of them, because I can't keep my eyes off this woman who has wormed her way into my brain.

Only now we're at an older home that has a sign out front advertising dog boarding, pet grooming, and… *Tarot readings*? Ashton's best friend might be the strangest person I've ever met in my life.

"She looks like a Dr. Seuss character!" Ashton cries as the poor collie walks out from the back of the house.

Her fur has been shaved to the skin everywhere except around her face and the bottoms of each paw. The pitiful animal's head droops, and even she looks humiliated.

"I didn't have a choice!" Lulu cries, storming in from the back of the house, dressed in a sexy nurse costume.

I have to give it to her, she's cute in that outfit. Her frizzy red hair is smoothed into two low ponytails on each side of her head, and the low-cut white dress shows off her ample cleavage. She even has one of those little hats on her head.

"Hey there, hot stuff." She stops at the sink near where I'm leaning against the wall out of the way and gives me a wink and a little *click-click* sound with her mouth. "How's it hanging?"

"Are you going to a birthday party?" I'm so confused.

"Process server." She steps back and straightens the top of her white, thigh-high panty hose. "Doctor hasn't made child support payments in a year. Asshole. The man has the money, and I'm about to let him know it's time to face the music."

My lips press into a frown. "I don't like process servers."

"Hardly anybody does." She shrugs, shoving a folded blue pamphlet in the side of her dress. "The way I see it, I'm making sure people do what's right, and I try to deliver the bad news along with a fun story they can tell their friends."

"I take it you've talked to my brother?" Ashton stands from where she was petting the scalped collie.

"I have." Lulu crosses her arms. "He's all upset about something. I guess it's a case he's working on? Someone's dodging his calls or not calling him back? I don't know."

"I'm sure that's making him a joy to be around." Ash rolls her eyes.

My stomach sinks at the mention of her brother. I've got to figure out a way to talk to her about all of this. She's just so damn pretty in that red dress, and the way she looked at me after I stood up to those bitches at the restaurant...

I couldn't do it then. I couldn't spoil her moment of triumph. I could only tell her the truth—my heart isn't in that work anymore. I'm not sure what to make of my heart these days.

"I don't know." A little smile curls Lulu's lips. "I'm pretty much always happy to be around Ben. More lately than ever."

"No!" Ashton gasps, and her friend shrugs.

"Let's just say he's being very attentive to my work."

Ashton surprises me with a laugh—they both collapse into each other laughing. "Miracles never cease!" Ashton cries, and Lulu suddenly stops, straightening.

"What the hell is that supposed to mean?"

"Clearly not what you're thinking. I just can't believe my *old* brother is learning *new* tricks. You're way too good for him."

"I don't know." Lulu straightens her hat before dashing over and pulling me into a hug. "I never thanked you for saving Jean Claude. You really are one of the good guys, Mr. Stud."

"That's Studly to you!" Ashton cups her hand around her mouth, calling after her.

"I don't have time to find out what that means. I'm headed out. Lock up when you leave."

The two say goodbye, and Ash turns back to me, her eyes shining with joy. She's so damn happy today. I go to her and catch her by the waist, pulling her body to mine. Fuck all that other shit weighing me down.

"Do I finally get to kiss you now?"

Her pretty hazel eyes are molten green mixing with warm brown. "You want to kiss me?" I love it when she's sassy.

"You have no idea." I'm leaning down, my lips ready to take hers, when fuck it all, my damn phone starts buzzing in my pocket again.

Ashton steps back and glances at my waist. Her bottom lip goes behind her teeth, and I pull the device out of my jeans pocket. Bernice's picture is on the screen, and I quickly silence it, shoving it back and stepping forward to pick up where we left off. The sink behind her looks about the right height to sit Ashton's cute little ass on, spread those legs, and fuck her good.

Only she takes another step away from me. Her arms are crossed, and she's frowning now, anger flashing in those eyes. "And who was that?"

"What?" My semi has switched my mind to one thing.

"That was a woman's picture on the screen. Don't tell me

she's some real estate deal. Who was that?"

"Oh," I exhale a laugh. "It's just my sister."

I'm moving toward her again, but she keeps stepping out of my reach. It's starting to make me crazy.

"Your sister." Her arms are still crossed and her eyes are narrowed. "As in the one with the kitten on the roof, three daughters, and no husband?"

"I never said she had no husband."

I don't want to talk about this. I want to sink into her warm depths. I want to slide my lips down the V of that dress to her soft breasts and suck, pull, bite. I want to bend her over and make her scream my name as she comes, throbbing and wet around my cock.

Ashton does a little skip away from me. "I want to meet her."

It's a cold bucket of water on my hot fantasy. "What?"

"I want to meet her." Ashton's arms are crossed, and even her defiant stance is adorably sexy. "I want to meet this mystery sister with the three kids, the kitten, and no husband."

"I never said she didn't have a husband, but if you insist..." A grin splits my cheeks as I close the space between us, catching her upper arms before she can step away from me again. "You're seriously messing up my plans for today."

"Don't change the subject." She tries to jerk her chin away, but I catch it with my fingers.

"Kiss me."

She fights the smile trying to curl her lips, but she doesn't pull away. She leans forward and attempts to give me a chaste, closed-lip kiss on the mouth. Don't worry, I turned that nonsense into something more.

THE RIGHT STUD

—

If Ashton thought she'd catch me in a lie, I have a feeling she's regretting that assumption. Molly, Mellany, and Mayla are all over her demanding to hear all about Jean Claude van Ram. Ashton sits on the couch with one triplet to her left, one to her right, and the third hanging over behind her.

"Do you have a picture of him?" Mellany cries, diving over the back of the couch toward her.

"No." Ashton shakes her head, unaffected by my middle-niece's dive bomb. "JC and I don't get along very well."

"Why ever not?" The oldest Molly's eyes are wide, and her leg is crossed. I can tell she's attempting to be very adult for their new guest. "I imagine he must be a very good goat to have such a great name."

Ashton doesn't miss a beat. "He's not."

"Has he ever eaten a tin can?" Mayla bounces nonstop at Ashton's right.

"He's eaten almost all of my flowers. The minute your uncle saved him, he was off sticking his head in my sweet olive."

"I've got to hand it to her." Bernice sidles up beside me, handing me a beer. "They overwhelm me when they get so wound up, and I'm their mother."

"Uncle Jax is a hero!" Mellany cries, diving over the back of the couch again. "He saved Mittens from the roof!"

"Mel!" Bernice shouts. "Stop jumping on the back of the couch. Sit in the chair."

Mellany's shoulders drop, and she stomps around to the armchair across from where my other two nieces are dominating Ashton's attention.

"Do you really live in a big shell by the sea?" Mayla is the youngest and definitely has the most vivid imagination.

"I wish!" Ashton leans back, and Mayla does the same. Molly stays upright with her leg crossed. "Then I'd be a real mermaid... or SpongeBob!"

"Uncle Jax said you live in a conch shell." Molly casts a disgusted look my way, as if I've treated her like a baby.

"It is called The Conch Shell," Ashton explains. "But it's just a regular house. Your uncle is helping me fix it up. Maybe you can come and stay with me one day."

"Oh!" Mellany is out of her chair and jumping up and down beside Bernice. "Can we, Mamma? Can we?"

"Let's let Uncle Jax finish what he's doing first." Mellany takes off running in the direction of the kitchen, and I mouth a thank you to my sister. She leans into my ear. "No problem. Now you nail this one down. She's a keeper for sure."

Mellany comes running back into the room holding Mittens in front of her in both hands. The kitten's front legs are extended, and she lets out a desperate *meow* when my niece stops in front of Ashton. "This is Mittens! She likes to get on the roof, but Uncle Jax can get her down."

"When Daddy's not in Boston. Now give Ashton room to breathe, girls." Bernice leaves me to rescue my date from the onslaught of love. "Head to the kitchen. Time for snacks."

"Snacks!" Mayla's next bounce is off the sofa and running after my sister to the kitchen.

The other two girls follow, and I take Molly's place on the couch. "You didn't believe me." It's a teasing accusation, and Ashton only shakes her head.

"I didn't." She actually laughs. "They're adorable."

"They're work."

"They love you." Her eyes narrow. "You're a hero."

The way she says it makes my dick twitch. "Let's get out of here. This hero is ready to get back to what I've been thinking about all day."

She wrinkles that cute little nose and leans closer. "I'll tell you a secret." Soft lips graze the shell of my ear, and my dick twitch turns into a semi in my pants. "I've been thinking about it all day, too."

Chapter 19

Ashton

A cool afternoon breeze is blowing in from the Atlantic as we leave Bernice's and walk back to the car, and the sound of sea gulls is prevalent even though we're three blocks from the beach.

The air smells likes gardenias, rich and spicy, and I inhale deeply.

Jax stares down at me as we walk along the sidewalk. "Happy?"

I pause mid-step but quickly recover with this hand on my arm, which noticeably slips down and curls into mine. My heart pounds at the electricity that sparks between us. *Happy?* Yes. But I'm terrified to tell him that. This is too much too soon, right?

I settle for sending him a sheepish grin. I really have had the most incredible day with him and his nieces, and I'm not ready for it to end. I'm like a kid at the fall carnival who doesn't want to get off the rollercoaster. Because Jax Roland *is* my rollercoaster. I feel euphoria when I look at him—I'm exhilarated but terrified at the same time. What if I fall off and break my neck? What if he sees a prettier girl at the fair and dumps me for her?

Arggg. Why do I care so much?

It's my heart. My heart can't handle anymore. Just seeing

Monica today brought back the memories of how Kyle lied to me. God, I'm a basket case. One minute I want him and the next I'm scared to death.

I toss his question back at him. "Are you happy?"

A pensive expression crosses his face as he pulls his eyes from mine and looks off into the distance. "I think so."

"You think so? What does that mean?"

He takes a deep breath, the inhalation causing me to notice his broad chest. He scratches at the afternoon shadow on his jawline. "I guess I haven't really been happy in a long time. I mean, I *thought* I was, but here, I feel different. Maybe for the past few years I've just been... existing."

I suck in a little breath, trying to play it cool, but I can't help but wonder what he means. "Can I ask you something?" I say.

"Anything."

"I know it's late in the game to even ask since we've already done the boom-boom, but you're not... seeing anyone back in New York, right?"

"Boom-boom?" He tosses his head back and a deep laugh erupts. "Ash, honey, call it like it was. It was fucking amazing."

I pretend to be offended. "Okay fine. We had glorious, mind-blowing, stupefying, inconceivable, staggeringly awesome sex."

"That's much better." He quickly sobers and lifts his hand to my face. Tilting my chin up, he stares deep into my eyes. "I'd never have slept with you if I was seeing anyone else. I'm not him."

"Kyle."

He nods. "He's a fucking asshole and if I ever see him again..."

I chew on my lip.

"Don't be having regrets about us, Ash." There's a vulnerability to him as he says the words, as if maybe he too is scared—although I can't imagine about what.

I remind myself we've only been together a few days, so why do I feel like I've known him my entire life? It's as if we've always had a connection, and it took us meeting at the Smoky Siren for Fate to finally bring us together.

"Come over here. Let me tell you a story." He leads me to a bench in the grassy area just off the square. We stroll together and damn if it doesn't feel like this is the way I'm supposed to be —with him on a lazy summer evening, walking and talking.

We sit and his hand plays with my fingers. "You asked if I was happy, and the thing is, I'm not sure I know what happy is. I know what it isn't. It isn't my mother pushing me out of my own house when I was just a kid. That whole experience…it made me never want to come back here."

"So you love New York? You're just a city boy through and through?"

He shakes his head. "I do love the city. I dig how vibrant it is and the fact that I can leave my apartment at two in the morning and still find a damn good slice of pizza or a great cup of coffee." He smirks. "I know I'm a tough guy with the hammer but I like to eat at five-star restaurants. I love The Met and Central Park. I like being around a lot of people. I thrive off of it. Probably because I'm an extrovert, and it's how I get my energy."

"I'm not…"

He puts a finger to my lips. "You didn't let me finish."

I nod.

"Being here for the past few days…soaking in all the scenery…" He sighs, and his gaze roams around, taking in one of my favorite historic houses on the square, a whitewashed two-story structure with beautiful Mediterranean blue hurricane shutters decorating the front. Deep window boxes stuffed with a riot of colorful flowers hang down from the top railing. He smiles a distant look on his face. "It feels different this time. I'm not thinking about my mom or how I can't wait to shake the dust from this place off my feet. I feel alive here and that's never happened."

Butterflies swarm in my stomach. "What do you mean?"

"I mean it's going to be hard to leave." He moves in closer. "The truth is, South Carolina has never made me happy...until you."

Chapter 20

Jax

A little gasp comes from her, and I take the opportunity to press my lips to hers…softly.

We kiss sweetly and her hand curls around my neck, fingers trailing through the hair at my nape. The kiss deepens and my hands brush over her breasts, seeking entry into the deep V of her dress.

In the distance, a horn blows, and both of us pull back, our eyes clinging.

I've loved kissing her since the moment we met, when I didn't even know who she was. Now, all I want to do is keep kissing her, especially when she smiles at me the way she is now.

A man in a suit on his cell walks past us, and I think of Ben. *Shit. What the hell am I going to do about him?* Do I really want to turn down a six-figure commission? Don't I need that money?

But…

I glance down at Ash, taking in her wide eyes and the eagerness on her face "What?" she asks.

"We need to talk about… something." My stomach tightens. Doubt creeps into my mind, pushing out the good stuff and leaving a knot of worry.

"Okay. What do we need to talk about?" Her head tilts to the side, and she's just so adorable.

I can't do it now—not yet. Not while she's looking at me, eyes glowing, like I'm her hero. She's all in with me. Somewhere between lunch and the triplets, she's decided to give me a shot, and I'm afraid I'm going to blow it.

I shove that thought away. I do more than shove it away. Hell, I pack it up in a chest, put a lock on it, and throw it out to sea.

Tucking a strand of hair behind her ears, I change directions. "I want to know everything about you."

She chuckles. "Everything?"

I nod. "Start at the beginning, the day you were born, how much you weighed and when you took your first steps."

A slow blush steals up her cheeks. "You'll be bored. I'm just a small-town girl who grew up here and never wanted to leave. I know every cobblestone street in this square. I know the couple that lives in that bungalow." She points to the older home with the flowers spilling off the balcony.

"Who lives there?"

"It's the Potter family and believe it or not the husband's name is Harry."

"Harry Potter? You're lying."

"I'm not."

"Is he married to Hermione?"

She giggles. "No, but he does have short dark hair and wears these little round glasses. He's the town doctor."

I smirk. "Dr. Harry Potter."

She points back to the house. "He has a son named Draco."

I burst out laughing. "Now you're just pulling my leg."

She laughs along with me, tears of merriment glistening in

her gaze. "Totally, but you should have seen your face when I said it."

I slip an arm around her shoulder, and we lean back and stare up at the sky. The sun is setting, and it's obvious we have work to do back at the house. Still, neither of us is in a hurry to get to it.

"I take it you're a J.K. Rowling fan?"

She nods. "You?"

"Slytherin all the way, baby."

She rolls her eyes. "I should have known you'd be a snake in the grass."

I grin. "Let me guess. You're a Hufflepuff?"

She narrows her eyes at me. "What gave it away?"

"Because you're beautiful, steady, and true."

Her mouth parts. "Oh."

"And after you called me a snake in the grass, I compliment you."

She playfully punches me on the shoulder. "Ah, can't you take a joke? Everyone knows that Slytherins are really Type-A people who love control and want to dominate."

I rake my eyes over her. "You got that right. I do like my control."

She bites her lip. "You're such a flirt!"

"Only with you."

"Liar. You're a total womanizer. Remember, I met you while you were on a date." She's teasing, of course, but I think I see a flicker of worry on her face as the words come out.

"It was a set-up. A blind date to make my sister happy. That's all."

"Right." She nods, looking off into the distance, and I want to kick myself. I try to steer things back to her... to us.

"I have an idea."

Her hazel eyes find mine.

"Let's head back to the house, hole up in my room and watch a movie."

"You really think we're going to 'watch a movie'?"

I shrug. "Why not? It's lady's choice. Whatever you want."

She gets a glint in her eye. "I've really been hankering for *Dirty Dancing*—the original."

Oh, no. All that dancing and shit.

My expression never changes.

She squints at me. "And I mean really watch it. It's one of the most romantic movies ever. It's a must-see for any American."

I raise my eyebrows. "Okay, you don't have to talk me into it. I watch *Beauty and the Beast* at least three times when I'm in town with the triplets. I think I can handle some smooth-talking Patrick Swayze."

"Nobody puts Baby in a corner." She studies my face, but I'm giving her my best poker face. "You don't even know what that means, do you?"

"No clue."

She's crestfallen. "But it's iconic! Even if you haven't seen the movie, you've seen clips of it, right?"

I shrug.

"We need to make a list of romantic movies you haven't seen, because I'm going to make you watch each and every one of them while you're staying with me." She pauses. "Have you see *The Notebook*?"

"Is it a football movie?

Her eyes roll. "Seriously, I have so much to teach you."

I grab her hand as we start walking. "Bring it."

We're passing by someone who knows Ashton, and she stops to say hi. My phone pings again with a new text, and thankfully, Ashton doesn't notice this time. I pull it out of my pants to check, and sure enough, it's Ben.

Been trying to call. Have you seen the house yet? I need to know the value ASAP. Call me.

Fuck. The pressure is back, and I know I have to talk to Ashton about this. I'd intended do it after we left Bernice's, but I got derailed by happiness and talking about New York and Harry Potter and boom-boom. Now we're going back to watch a movie she's all excited about—in my bed.

Just tell her tomorrow.

Tomorrow is a whole new day.

I want this day—this night—to be perfect.

Turning my phone off, I shove it deep into the pocket of my jeans as she turns.

"Ready?"

I nod, and we head to the car, our hands laced together.

Chapter 21

Ashton

It's after midnight, and I'm lying in Jax's arms in his bed. He's twirling a piece of my hair around his fingers, and our feet are tangled together as we rest on top of the duvet.

Yeah, we never even made it to pulling back the sheets once we giggled our way up the stairs and into his room. After the first round of lovemaking, we made our way to the shower where Jax washed every single inch of me—with his tongue.

God. That tongue.

The man has *talents*.

While part of me knows he probably got those talents from being with other women, I refuse to think about it and just focus on the moment. I'm done with waffling around and having second thoughts. I think…I think I'm all in with him. I want this thing we have. I want him even if it's only for a week or so…but I don't let my head go there. Our future is uncertain, yes, but all my chips are on the table. I pray I don't lose everything.

Dirty Dancing is on the TV across from the bed, and it's the final big dance scene where Johnny and Baby are on stage. I peek up at Jax, and he's watching with a wry smile on his handsome face. The song "Time of my Life" is playing, and the familiar beat makes me giddy. A huge smile is on my face.

I teasingly pop him on the arm. "You're judging my all-time favorite movie, aren't you?"

His piercing blue eyes find mine. "Maybe."

"But isn't it so... perfect? The dresses are amazing, the hair styles are on point, and the cheesy dialogue is the best." I pause. "And you have to admit, for an eighties movie, it covered some deep topics: abortion, divorce, social prejudices. Why, this movie was ahead of its time! It's more than just a classic. It's freaking *art*."

His chest moves just a little as he laughs, and I pout at him. Which only seems to make him chuckle more, making my head on his shoulder bounce.

"You're just jealous you don't have moves like Patrick Swayze." I throw him a side-eye, which is hard to do when you're stark naked, and your body is pressed tight against the most magnificent male specimen alive. For a brief moment, I let my eyes eat up his tan chest, the dusting of curls there, the deep V where his hips meet his pelvis. God had definitely been on his A-game when he created Jax Roland.

I pluck at one of his chest hairs and hold it hostage, making him yelp. "Come on," I say. "Just admit that you love the damn movie."

"I love the movie," he deadpans—then bursts out laughing.

I scowl. "Now you're really hurting my feelings. I mean, just look at Baby's face! Look at Johnny's. They're in love..." I let out a sigh.

Jax stops laughing and cups my cheek, turning me toward him until we're eye to eye. Electricity crackles in the room, and I can feel this weird connection we have rising to the surface, igniting my instinct to once again let him completely devour me. My chest rises and my voice is whisper-soft. I say what's in my heart. "I want someone to love me like he loves her."

A torn expression flits across his face, and his thumb strokes across my bottom lip. "You will, Ash."

My heart skips a beat. "How do you know?"

I think I want him to say, *Because you're my Baby, and I'll be your Johnny*...but he doesn't.

He curls a roped bicep around my shoulder and pulls me closer. "Because you deserve the fucking world."

Chapter 22

Ashton

The next morning around six, I roll out of Jax's bed, give him a quick snuggle and a hurried kiss—morning breath and all, since he refused to let me leave otherwise. With a quick murmur about getting breakfast started, I finally sneak out and tiptoe back to my room.

Once I'm showered and dressed in a flowy yellow sundress, I head downstairs to make coffee and bake muffins. When Jax is ready to start today's renovations, I'll change into work clothes.

Lost in thought, I don't even hear Mrs. C enter the kitchen until Rufus flaps his wings and heads to his perch.

I whip around, and she's standing regally in the middle of the room wearing her multi-colored pajamaralls and a tropical printed turban. I blink at the brightness.

"Mornin'!" She gives me a wide grin. "Did I hear *Dirty Dancing* last night?"

I busy myself getting cups from the cabinet, only giving her a slight shrug.

"I knew it!" she exclaims. "I can tell by that pleased as punch look on your face. That's the second time you've gotten the Big D. Should I start making baby plans?"

I gasp. "Really, Mrs. C?"

She waves me off. "Mercury's in retrograde. It makes us all horny. Even Rufus here. Why he squawked all night long. Once I even caught him grinding against the cage. Damn bird."

"Fuck!" comes from Rufus. "Bacon!"

I sigh. Clearly I need to invest in soundproofing upstairs. Maybe a noise machine in the hallway by the stairs.

Does that mean you plan on having lots of sexy nights with Jax? my head asks.

Yes. Yes, it does, and I couldn't be happier about it.

Mrs. C pulls open the fridge and grabs the container of already cooked bacon. Her face is all dreamy when she straightens. "I can just see the pretty babies you two would make. The pitter patter of little feet is just what this old place needs."

"That's silly!" My neck feels hot, and I turn quickly to hide the little smile trying to curl my lips. Jax *would* make the most beautiful babies…

"Why?" She breaks the pork into small pieces, tossing a few to Rufus, who barely moves a muscle catching them. "It ain't over til it's over, and the way you two have been going at it…" She sighs. "Makes me miss Mr. C."

Rufus's beady eyes are on me as he starts bobbing his body, his scratchy voice singing out "Time of my life." I nearly giggle but bite it back. For once, I'm feeling rather affectionate toward the darn bird, so I give him a little smirk.

"See, even he knows what's going on. You're fooling no one, so just admit it." Mrs. C pours a liberal amount of creamer in her cup and stirs it.

I plop down at the table and take a long sip of coffee. "He is something," I sigh, unable to deny the happiness bubbling in my chest any longer. "I never thought I'd be able to trust a man again."

"Kyle is an asshole." She straightens in her chair, nodding to me in a knowing way. "That man up there is hot as sin, and no one can blame you. You deserve it!"

"What does she deserve?" The male voice is loud and a bit annoyed.

Great. Ben is here.

"Good morning to you, too." I stand and breeze past him to the sink.

I haven't spoken to my brother since he was here a few days ago, and my feelings of anger still simmer just beneath the surface. "I didn't hear the doorbell ring or I would have let you in."

"I let myself in." Ben is dressed in a sharp navy suit with a perfectly coordinated tie. "I do have a key, you know, and I am half-owner of this house."

I inhale deeply. *Don't get sucked into arguing with him.* You catch more flies with honey, and if there's one thing I must do, it's convince him to give up his silly idea of selling this house and razing it to the ground.

My blood pressure rises at the thought of seeing a high-rise condo sitting on the beach where I grew up.

Before I know it, my arms are crossed, and I'm staring daggers at him. I've always looked up to my brother. He's a sharp lawyer and has made quite a name for himself in Palmetto, but he's not sentimental. He wasn't close to Granny like I was.

"So what's the reason for your early visit?" I ask.

His eyes move from me to Mrs. C, who's currently devouring a muffin.

"You looking for Lulu?" A few crumbs are on her chin, and she wipes at them, her gaze steely as she rakes it up and down him.

He stiffens, straightening to his full height. "Why would I be looking for her?"

"I see things, and I know things." She taps her head. "Don't underestimate this old lady. My mind is a steel trap. The only thing that makes me crazy and wild is the smell of serrano peppers cooking because it reminds me of Mr. C and our fun times..."

She goes on a bit about how Mr. C would feed them to her, and my ears get hot, when Ben cuts her off. "Okay, great." He stares back at me, a determined look on his face.

"So, you and Lulu?" I say, just to irk him.

He glowers at me, and now he's the one crossing his arms. "No! How many times do I have to say it?"

"Then why are you here?"

He juts out his jaw. "I asked someone to come and appraise the house. He should have been here yesterday or the day before."

Anger flashes in my gut. "Who?" My fists are clenched at my sides.

He rolls his eyes. "Don't get pissed, Ashton. I told you I wanted someone to come out and make an offer or at least give us an estimate. This isn't news, and I mean, just look at this place. It needs a complete overhaul—something you can't afford to do."

He looks around at the kitchen, and I know what he's doing, adding up figures in his head.

"I can make it work!"

"No, you can't." His voice is maddeningly calm, and it ratchets up my fury.

"You can't sell this house. I won't let you."

"You can't stop me." He pulls out his phone, muttering under his breath. "I can't believe this guy was a no-show, especially when he knew how big the commission would be."

I feel a tic in my eye and rub it. "You're not as smart as you think you are. Maybe this place isn't worth what you think it is."

He lets out a grunt and shows me his phone. "See, it's right here. Jax Roland with Pearson Real Estate. We met for coffee on Sunday, and he assured me he'd come here and—"

"What?" The room tilts, and I steady myself, placing my hand on the closest wall. "Did you say Jax... Roland?"

Shuffling comes from behind me, and I spin around. Jax is standing there dressed for work, but his eyes widen when he sees my brother. His face goes white.

His gaze darts from me to Ben and back again. "Ashton... I can explain."

The air is sucked out of the room, and the coffee I had earlier threatens to come up. *This.* This is it. Just when I put my trust in someone, I get the rug pulled right out from under me.

"You're working with my brother?" My chest squeezes, and I rub at it. "All this time you acted like you were helping me... You came here to *evaluate* my house to see what it's worth?"

Jax rakes a hand through his hair, his expression torn. "Yes, but it's not what you think—"

"Wait... You're staying here?" In my peripheral vision, I see Ben's hand go to his hip, but I can't take my eyes off the man I spent the night with.

The man I spent all week with, tearing out old boards and adding new ones, painting, filming, teasing... Getting to know him, talking to him about everything, preparing my best recipes, kissing in the kitchen, making love... Mrs. C's comments, the pretty babies... *I never thought I'd be able to trust a man again...*

"Now you've done it." Mrs. C's voice is quiet.

"What the fuck?" Ben's sharp voice cuts through the tension in the air. "Is that why you've been ignoring my calls?"

In a flash I remember all the calls Jax ignored—and every time he ignored them.

"You lied to me." I can't believe how calm my voice sounds. My insides feel like the burning of Atlanta, giant buildings falling down, ablaze with destruction. He destroyed it all.

Jax clears his throat. "It wasn't like that. I didn't meet Ben until after I came here."

I shake my head no. I can't swallow. I can't breathe, and I sure as hell can't stay in this room another minute. I will not cry. Not in front of my brother, and definitely not in front of Jax. Taking a step away, I raise my hand, fighting tears with every fiber of my being.

"Ashton, wait. Let me explain." Jax takes a step toward me, but my vision has blurred.

Turning fast, I run out of the kitchen, heading for the stairs. My feet thump loudly as I fly up them as fast as I can, going straight to my room.

Inside, I pace, shaking my hands and taking deep breaths. My entire body is trembling, and it feels like the walls are closing in around me.

A traitorous sniff jerks my chest, and I want my grandmother. I go to the closet. Pulling the door open, I drop to my hands and knees and crawl inside to where I'm surrounded by the lingering scent of her clothes. With my back against the wall, I look up at my mural, at Ariel, the girl who has everything.

My throat is so tight it aches, and with a blink, the first hot tear hits my cheek. Jax was my secret weapon. He was supposed to help me fix up the place and show Ben I was right, show him I could make it work here. He answered my email and said he'd help me—I remember that day so vividly, my elation, my happiness, my optimism.

It's a concrete block in my chest.

My knees are bent, and I shove my hands into the sides of my hair. All the money, the debt I accumulated from my failed wedding, the cost of replacing the roof, the repairs that still need to be done. I'm losing, and I feel it all slipping through my fingers. I'm sliding down the cliff with no one to extend a hand or even break my fall.

"I tried so hard, Granny…" The words escape on a broken whisper. "What do I do now?"

Kyle's betrayal broke my heart, but it's only now, sitting here on the brink of losing everything that I realize how much he cost me. I'd reached out to Jax, and he'd said he'd help me… Then he did the same thing.

My fists tighten on my knees, and a growl rises in my chest. *No. Not again.* I'm not lying down and letting another man do this to me. No more Miss Nice Girl. My nose is hot and my face is slick with tears, but I push off the floor. Throwing the closet door open, I come out in a blaze of fury.

Voices rise from the foyer downstairs as I make my way down the hall, across the landing, headed to Jax's room. I don't even hesitate. I fling open his door and storm inside. With a pause, I take in the clothes scattered around, the toiletries in the bathroom, the shoes on the floor.

"Not in my house." My voice is husky and wild.

"Ashton?" My brother calls from downstairs. "Stop being stubborn and come down here and talk."

The inferno in my chest has spread to my brain, and all I can think is *Actions speak louder than words*. Going to the window, I raise the blinds with a jerk. The window is already open, and I unfasten the screen, pushing it out of the way.

From there, I go to the shoes lined along the wall and scoop them up, throwing them out the window. They fall onto the scrub below with a thump. Next, I pull Jax's clothes off the hangers in the closet and ball them up in my arms. Shoving them out the window, I only pause a moment to watch them spread like sails before drifting slowly to join the shoes on the ground.

"Fuck!" I hear Rufus croak. "It's raining men!"

Adrenaline drives me, and I go to the bathroom, scooping up all his toiletries and running to the window to throw them all out. My eyes light on the desk, and I see his laptop, the digital camera he used to film me while I worked, the same one I used to film him while I dreamed of how beautiful we'd make this old house.

It's the biggest betrayal of all, and I snatch it up, moving fast to the window.

"What are you doing?" Jax's voice is loud from the door, and his feet thud across the floor. "Stop!"

I'm at the window, ready to throw the camera out, followed closely by his laptop, but large hands grip my upper arms, preventing me.

"Let me go!" I shout, twisting side to side, trying to get out of his grasp. "Take your hands off me, Liar!"

"Ashton." His deep voice is sharp, commanding. "Stop this!"

With a forceful jerk, I'm out of his grip. "You're worse than Kyle," I shout, my chest rising and falling rapidly. "He broke my heart, but you... you acted like you cared about my dreams. You said you wanted to help me."

His blue eyes flash. "I do want to help you. You're not giving me a chance to explain—"

"You're damn right I'm not. I've given you all the chances you'll ever get from me. Now I want you out... GET OUT!"

Chapter 23

Jax

Fuck.

My chest is tight, and every muscle in my body is tense. Betrayal flashes in Ashton's eyes, and every word is a lash ripping across my heart. She stands in front of the window, holding my camera against her heaving breast, shouting at me to leave.

I'm trying to stay calm, but it's almost impossible. "I won't leave this way. You have to let me explain."

She makes another dash toward the window, and I lunge forward to intercept her. Downstairs, I'd been trying to explain to Ben when we both saw my things raining down on the lawn. That damn bird shouted out what was going on, and I ran up here to stop her.

"I won't let you have any of it. You can't steal my dreams." Her voice trembles like her body as she tries to throw my camera out the window.

"No!" I grab the three-thousand-dollar device out of her hand. "You can't break my camera."

Her eyes flash, and my hands drop, holding the expensive piece of equipment. "Why not?" Her voice is sharp, and she's breathing hard, her hair flying around her face.

I must be insane, because I think she is so beautiful right now, fiery and wild. "I can't afford to replace it."

"You can't afford…" Her slim brows furrow. "You said you'd do the show, all the repairs, the supplies… How can you do that if you can't even afford a camera?"

"We don't have the budget." Guilt is heavy in my tone. "I was hoping this job would be something I could use to take us to the next level."

She shakes her head and walks away from me. It's like my insides are torn out, lying on the floor, all of it laid bare.

"So it was all a lie. Every single thing you said to me was a lie." She's pacing again, and I see her fury rising. Her hazel eyes flash like emeralds mixed with lava. "You're not a hero. You're just like Kyle."

"No—"

"What's going on up here?" Ben has joined us, his voice loud and commanding from the door. "Ashton, stop this behavior at once. What is wrong with you?"

"I'm not talking to you!" she snaps at her brother.

"Yes, you are!" he snaps right back. Gotta love siblings. "This behavior is ridiculous—and completely unprofessional. We made an agreement to see what we could get for the place. You're being stubborn like always."

"I am not!" Ashton's voice is pure indignation and self-defense. "He lied to me."

"I don't know anything about that." Ben turns to me, smoothing his hands down the front of his jacket. "Jax, tell her what you've observed in your time here."

A knot is in my throat, and I try to swallow it away. It's impossible when I see the tornado of emotions on Ashton's face, the remnants of tears on her cheeks. Just last night she was in my arms. We watched *Dirty Dancing*, and lying on my back, I'd tried to lift her with my hands and feet... What did she call it? *Coming in hot?* She only ended up collapsed on my chest, both of us laughing until we started kissing then making love...

She shifts her weight to one foot, cocking out a hip and crossing her arms. "Yes, Jax Roland." She says my name like it's acid on her tongue. "What have you observed in your time here?"

I don't want to do this. I take a deep breath, but it doesn't help. It's like knives stabbing my lungs. "He's right, Ashton." My voice is quiet, but firm. I won't lie to her, regardless of what she thinks of me now. "This place is a maintenance nightmare. You'll never be able to keep up with the cost of repairs. They'll eat into any profit you might make running a B&B here."

She sniffs and straightens her back, fighting my words with good posture. Fuck, I can't stand to see her this way, blinking fast, refusing to cry the tears I put in her eyes.

"Is that so." It's not a question. It's a wavering statement of defiance.

"You know it's so," Ben cuts in, impatient and ignorant of what's going on between us, what's crumbling to pieces. "Now stop acting like a spoiled brat."

"You care nothing about your family!" she fires back, pointing her finger at his chest.

"Ashton..." he groans, turning to me. "Tell her, Jax."

"I won't lie to you." My voice is quiet. "You'll make more money selling this house than you ever will keeping it."

Her teeth clench behind her tight lips, and her eyes blink faster. Boldness flashes all over her body like invisible armor. "Thank you for your opinion."

Ben is quick to interject. "It's not his opinion. It's the facts."

"I'll give you a fact." Her voice is low, and I confess, a little scary. "I'm never selling Granny's house. *Never!* Sue me if you want. I'm not letting you in here, and I'm never letting you condemn it. Now get out."

"You can't tell me to get out." Ben exhales a frustrated chuckle.

"I just did. I want both of you out of my house. Now. Get out!"

With a screech like a banshee, something flies into the room on cerulean blue wings.

"Get the fuck out!" Rufus shoots through the doorway and starts flying in a circle, diving at Ben's head. "Get the fuck out!"

The bird grasps with long claws, and Ben bats him away, waving his arms. "What the hell?" He ducks out the door, Rufus hot on his tail. "Mrs. Capshaw! Where are you? Put this bird in a cage." Ben jogs down the stairs shouting over Rufus's squawks. "It's a lawsuit waiting to happen."

Turning to face Ashton, my insides twist when I see the cold calm now on her features. It's worse than her fiery anger.

"Ashton." My voice is quiet, pleading. "Talk to me."

Her chin lifts, and she pushes past me to the door. "It should take no more than ten minutes for you to collect your things and get out of my house." Her tone is ice, and her hazel eyes flash as she casts me a final glance. "I'll give you five."

She leaves, and I drop to the bed.

What the fuck do I do now?

—

"Wait." Bernice paces the room, arms crossed. "I'm confused. Did you come here to help her save her house or did you come here to save your show... Or to make a fat commission?"

I'm on my sister's couch, elbows on my knees, rubbing my temples. "I came here for a fucking vacation."

"Don't get snippy with me." She shoves a tumbler of scotch into my hand. "Whatever you were thinking, you royally fucked it up."

"Thanks, sis." It's only 10 AM, but I need a stiff drink, and as much as I love my nieces, I'm glad they had a birthday-party-slash-sleepover last night.

I need a minute of quiet to get my head together and figure out what to do.

My sister sits beside me, her voice noticeably gentler. "Tell me what happened."

"I answered an email." Shaking my head, I try to quell the memories. "I thought I could use her house on the show. Tara said we needed more money, but I didn't even know about the commission when I got here."

"So it was an unlucky series of events?"

Was it unlucky? I think all the way back to that first night at the Smoky Siren.

Fate.

I don't believe in fate.

"She needed help." My voice is rough. "She asked me to come here and help her save her house. When I told her I could..."

I'll never forget how happy she was, her spontaneous hug followed by a quick apology. She was so damn cute, and that kiss... the memory of that kiss had me ready to do anything for more.

Contrast it to today. I can still see her shaking with anger, betrayal. I can still see the hurt in her eyes.

"You told her you'd help her... and what?"

"I fucked it up." Lifting the tumbler, I shoot what's in the glass.

My sister studies me with blue eyes identical to mine. She's sizing me up. "That's not like you. What happened?"

Swallowing the lump in my throat, I fight back against these emotions. "Too much... not enough. I got caught up in their family drama, and now I'm the bad guy."

"The bad guy who's drinking at ten in the morning?" I don't answer her right away, and after a few more minutes, she exhales and leans back, crossing her arms. "I saw it when you brought her here. That girl is special, and you know it."

My eyes squeeze shut, and I try to deny her words. Only I can't. Ashton *is* special.

"She's sweet." My voice is resigned. "She's smart, and I liked her house for the show. It would've been good for ratings, maybe even something my producer could pitch to the network."

"You liked her house." I glance over my shoulder, and her eyes are narrowed. "You liked the girl. She got under your skin."

Staring into my empty tumbler, I insist in my head she's wrong. I haven't fallen for Ashton. I only feel this way because it was a nice place. Mrs. C was a character, and the sex was good.

Okay, the sex was better than good. The sex was fucking amazing, and Ashton was... *is* a big part of the reason.

Still, I haven't changed. I'm the same guy I always was. I don't do relationships. I don't get hung up on women. I'm the *live and let live* guy. Free and easy. No strings.

If I'd made it to the end of the week, finished what I'd started, I wouldn't feel this way. It's the abrupt ending, the shock that has me second-guessing myself. "I need a glass of water."

"Help yourself."

Pushing against my knees, I stand and go to the kitchen. I place the tumbler on the counter and rub my fingers against my eyes.

It's more than that.

Ashton trusted me, and knowing I did this to her hurts more than I could have imagined.

"Hey." Bernice touches my shoulder, and I straighten, lowering my hand. "You okay? I confess, I'm a little worried. I've never seen you this way."

Clearing my throat, I relent. "It was more than the house." My confession is quiet.

Bernice, by contrast, is optimistic. "So what are you going to do about it?"

Glancing at her, I don't miss the light in her eyes. She thinks I have a chance. She has no idea.

"I need to apologize, but I know she won't see me."

"Only one way to find out." My sister is practically bouncing on the balls of her feet, and I know seeing me this way, actually caring deeply about a woman, is a dream come true for her.

"She threw me out, Bernie. As in, she literally threw my stuff out the window of my upstairs room. Then she sent her attack parrot after us."

A snort bursts from my sister. "She has an attack parrot?"

I wince at the memory. "Technically, no. But the bird knew what was going on. I should be smarter than a dumb bird."

Although, that's not entirely fair. Rufus is weirdly smart, now that I think about it.

"Listen to me." Bernice puts both hands on my shoulders, facing me as if I'm headed off to war. "If I were a girl, and you showed up on my doorstep with that face and that ass begging me for forgiveness, *trust me,* I'd forgive you."

"She's not you, and you haven't been through the shit storm life has dealt her this year. Ashton is not interested in my apologies."

She tilts her head to the side. "You never know until you try. What's the worst that could happen?"

"I don't know." After this morning, it could be anything.

At the same time, this pain in my stomach is driving me to her. I need to tell her I never wanted to displace her or Mrs. C. I never wanted to crush her dreams. I really did want to save her house. I really was happy here… if only she'd believe me.

Bernice gives my shoulder a gentle shake. "Just try."

Chapter 24

Ashton

Tape still guards the freshly painted boards on the porch, and I stand for a moment gazing at how pretty these small repairs have made the place.

I spent the last hour sitting on the floor in my closet. My head was either on my knees or pressed against the wall as I turned this sudden change of events over and over in my mind.

Now my stomach is a tight knot of anger, pain, anxiety... and determination. This time I've been pushed too far. This time I'm not walking away without a fight. What other choice do I have?

Walking around the curved, wooden porch, I pull down the tape, balling it in my hands. A cool, salty breeze blows through the open space, and my breath catches in my throat as memories bubble to the surface—the joy I felt pulling out the rotten boards, the optimism at seeing the fresh, new wood just waiting to be coated in paint.

We got about halfway through the exterior repairs, and it already looks so good. I can still imagine how it will look with everything finished, the doors open wide to new guests, couples strolling through the breezeway hand in hand or sitting in one of those rocking chairs sipping coffee or cool rosé, depending on the hour. It's my dream, and I'll be damned if I give up on it.

The floor creaks behind me, and I glance up to see Mrs. C making her way to where I stand. She's still in her pajamaralls, that turban on her head, and she stops beside me, looking out at the ocean, those deep blue waves that never stop rolling no matter how bad things get up here on dry land.

"Your grandmother loved this big ole porch." A smile curls her lips and crinkles her eyes. "She wanted to do everything out here, eat, paint, sit. I think she'd have slept out here if she'd had a hammock."

Stepping up to the rail beside her, I look out at the water. "When I was little, she'd set up a card table, and we'd play canasta and hearts."

"She was a whiz at gin rummy, beat me every time. Of course, I accused her of cheating." The old lady beside me chuckles then shakes her head. "She'd be real proud of what you're doing with the place."

My throat hurts, and the sadness in my chest threatens to spill out of my eyes again. I blink it away. "I never thought I'd be glad to see Rufus swooping in like he did this morning."

"Oh," she laughs more. "He knows some key phrases. *Get out* is one of them. He's a damn nuisance half the time, but I like to think he's there when I need him."

"Apparently male animals are the only males worth anything." The bitterness in my voice is unmistakable.

Mrs. C pats my arm. "The human variety aren't so bad. They just take a lot more patience."

"I'm all out of patience."

The sound of a car pulling into the gravel drive causes our eyes to meet. I'm frowning, but Mrs. C doesn't seem surprised. A door closes, and whoever it is jogs up the steps to the front door.

"That had better not be my brother," I growl, marching past my one guest to where whoever is about to start knocking. My stomach plunges, and I shuffle to a stop when I see Jax standing there.

His fist is raised to knock, and when he sees me, it lowers slowly. He turns to face me, not moving forward but not retreating either.

"Why are you back?" Anger burns in my chest, and I don't care how good he looks with his chin down, lifting those blue eyes to mine.

"Ashton." His deep voice is contrite, but I refuse to let it affect me.

"I told you to leave."

"I know." He glances at my bare feet, and I cross my arms over the pain in my chest. "I'll leave. I just—I need you to let me explain first."

"If I've got the timeline right, you had days to explain."

He nods. "I should have told you sooner—"

"You should have told me immediately."

He takes a step toward me, and I take a step back. He stops. "You're right, and when I didn't, I never could find the right time."

"I can think of several times you could have told me."

"Telling you the truth about this place was never going to be easy."

"So you lied to me—"

"I never lied."

"Not telling me something as important as what you were really doing here is the same as lying."

"I was trying to figure out a way to change things." His

voice rises, and I resist the flash of emotion it sends through my body. "When I said I wanted to help you, I meant it. I still want to help you, Ashton."

"No thank you." My chin lifts, and defiance shines in my eyes. "I'll take care of this myself. I don't need help from men who lie."

His fists clench at his sides, and he exhales a growl. "Stop saying that. Things were going really well. We were having fun, and I didn't want to spoil it."

Pain twists in my chest, but my broken heart fights back. "My home and I are not a game. You might have been having fun here, getting footage for your show, doing... whatever, but this is serious to me."

"You think I didn't take you seriously?"

He holds out his hands, and his expression, his eyes, all of it is killing me inside. "I have no idea what you take seriously. I thought you were one thing, and I was wrong. Now I want you to leave."

"Ashton—"

"No!" My voice rises. "This is a family matter, and you've interfered enough. This discussion is over. Go away, Jax."

If he were one of Lulu's dogs, his tail would be between his legs, but I can't worry about that. I also can't argue with him anymore. It hurts too much, and I have to take care of me now. Turning on my heel, I walk away, leaving him at the front door.

I'm not looking back. I have to regroup and figure out how I'm going to salvage my plan to save this house. I'll sort out my broken heart later.

Chapter 25

Ashton

Three Days Later

"Wear the red dress," Lulu says as she watches me rifle through my walk-in closet.

Clothes litter the room, shoes are piled up on my ottoman at the foot of my bed, and makeup is scattered across my vanity. After wallowing for three days, living in my pajamas, eating pints of Ben & Jerry's "Cake My Day," and watching *Dirty Dancing* (Yes, I'm a glutton for punishment, so sue me.), my best friend demanded I leave the house. This time, she's taking charge of my girl's night rebound.

My lips compress. "Not that red one. It's the one I wore when I met He-Who-Must-Not-Be-Named." I sigh. "He's a Slytherin. I should have known he was bad news."

Lulu toys with a strand of her hair. Wavy and long, she's ironed it smooth as red silk draping over her shoulders. "You referenced The Stud. That means you have to drink!"

I chuckle as she heads over to the nightstand and pours me another glass of prosecco from the bottle she'd brought up to my room from the kitchen. "They say bubbles get you drunker faster. Proven scientific fact."

"Let's hope." I take a swig and crank up the speaker that's

connected to my cell. Beyoncé's "Irreplaceable" blasts through the room and Lulu starts singing and dancing, her movements theatrical. She's doing her best to cheer me up.

I nod. *Hell yeah.* Screw Jax Roland and his lying heart. I don't need him. We're having a *killer* girls' night, and I'm determined to look amazing as hell. My bruised and battered ego demands it.

Beyoncé belts out the best girl-power, breakup song ever, and I'm getting pumped as I yank the most expensive dress I own off the rack—a shimmery blue mini dress with spaghetti straps and iridescent rhinestones on the bodice. The fabric is delicate with a lace overlay, and it shows most of my legs, making me look tall and willowy, even more so when I slip on a pair of four-inch silver stilettos.

Purchased with Kyle, this dress was meant for our honeymoon. I'm mildly surprised when that bit of information doesn't even make my heart twinge as I snip off the price tag. I twist and turn as I take in my image in the mirror. With my dark hair falling in loose waves down my back, I'm a mermaid.

Lulu grins her approval as she does a pirouette and jazz hands to the music. I snort a laugh, bracing against my dresser. The girl has skills, but I'm pretty sure Beyoncé never did jazz hands.

I think back to when Lulu showed up at my door, determined to talk me into going to the Smoky Siren. It pains me to think of going there again and not seeing Jax, but I'm sick of being in a funk over his betrayal. I have to move on. Plus, Lulu says she might have a new boarder for me, one of the servers at the bar.

It seems fruitless to even consider taking on someone else besides Mrs. C, especially since Ben is bearing down hard, but part of me, that piece of my soul that's always been a fighter, refuses to give up on my dream.

My brother has been calling and texting me, wanting to discuss the particulars of selling, but I refuse to respond. I'm pretending I can still make my plan work, even though I'm flat broke, way over my head in debt. Basically, I'm an ostrich, sticking my head in the sand or Jean Claude van Ram playing dead in the ocean.

And dammit if that doesn't bring to mind Jax diving into the ocean to save him. I recall how the water had dripped down his chiseled chest and to the deep V in his obliques…

Stop, Ashton!

Tears prick at my eyes and I blink them away. It's been so long since I've seen him, and nothing has been the same since.

Don't think about him.

I suck in a fortifying breath, gathering myself and digging deep for a mental pep talk.

You've got this, Ashton.

You WILL forget about him.

But…will I?

A pang strikes my chest, and I clutch the dresser, needing to feel grounded because every time his name flashes in my head, hurt slices through me.

How much longer until this horrible feeling of missing him disappears? What if it never does?

He hurt you, I remind myself. *He betrayed you. He's not worthy your love…*

Love?

God. I straighten up and push the thought away. Where did that come from? I can't even go *there*. I. Just. Can't.

At least for tonight, I'm going to pretend I never even met him.

"Your dress is slut-tastic," Lulu says with an eyebrow waggle.

I grimace. "It's the dress I bought for our fancy dinner in Oahu."

"Oh. I forgot about your honeymoon. You looked forward to that trip for a year. Are you okay?"

I wave her off. "Kyle is a distant memory. Douchebag Stud replaced him." My voice is bitter.

She puts her hands on her hips and sends an angry glare out the window, as if that's where He-Who-Must-Not-Be-Named is, when in fact, I have no clue where Jax went after I threw him out. I hope he's holed up in a Motel 6 with rubber eggs and day-old bagels. No bacon or blueberry muffins or flaky biscuits or fancy quiches for him!

With a sigh, I acknowledge he's probably staying with Bernice and those three little cuties. Saving a kitten… Or back in Manhattan, living the life.

That concrete block is in my chest again, and my bestie refills my glass as her phone pings with a text. I watch her pick it up from the bed and read it, her face brightening.

Her eyes dart up to me then back to her phone. Chewing on her lip, she types out a reply and then returns to me.

My brow lowers as I study the flowy lilac dress she's wearing that perfectly complements her bright red hair. Smoky eye shadow is on her lids, and if I'm not mistaken, it appears she's gone the extra mile to get ready—definitely more than she usually does for girls' night.

"What's going on with you?" I ask. "Are those eyelash extensions you're wearing?"

She flutters the black wing-like things at me. "I'm stoked that you noticed."

"You don't usually go to such lengths when we go out." Heck most of the time, she just does a swipe or two of gloss and mascara. "Anyone special you think you might be seeing?"

A slow blush starts at her neck and works up to her carefully made-up face. "Uh, no… Well…" Her voice drifts off, a hesitant expression on her face as she looks at her phone.

I cock my head. "Lulu? What aren't you telling me?"

She bites her bottom lip, obviously in distress, and then blurts out the words in a rush. "Ben texted me just now and said he's staying in to watch a movie and if I wasn't busy tonight I could come over. Of course, I told him I'd stop by after—"

"Ben!" I mean, I know she has a thing for him, but this is the first I've heard of him inviting her over to watch a movie. My hands flutter as I suck in a breath. "He asked you over? Are you *dating* him?"

Her face goes from blushing to pale. "We've messed around."

My mouth drops open, and I struggle for words. "You mean… you did the dirty?"

Her hands twist in front of her. "A little."

"Since when?" How long has everyone I know been hiding shit from me?

Lulu paces around the room. "It was a spur-of-the-moment thing in his office last week, and I swear it was that nurse's outfit; you know the one—"

"I know the one!" Emotion churns in my gut, and I rub my temples.

I've gone from being pumped to pissed in a matter of seconds, and my short fuse has everything to do with people letting me down.

"Don't be mad, Ashton. Please." A tiny wrinkle lines her

forehead, and she drops her chin, picking at her fingernail. "I really like him. You know I've always had a crush on him, even though it's a big no-no to fall for your best friend's brother. He's just so…" She shoots me a look under her lashes. "Hot."

My bestie has crossed to the enemy's side.

"*Et tu, Brute*?" I say. "Just let me get this knife out of my back here, and we'll go to the bar—or not—and you can rush over to Ben's."

She strides over to me, a torn expression on her face. "No, no. I want to go out. I can see Ben afterwards. I just want to be upfront about everything that's going on between us since you're upset with him."

Upset? I'm furious with him. He wants to take my home away from me—our grandmother's home. Fighting frustration, I look in the mirror that's over my dresser and brush my long hair, arranging the beach waves.

Lulu watches me anxiously. "Are you terribly mad at me?"

I study her, my best friend since kindergarten at Palmetto Elementary School. She's been right here with me through everything—my parents moving to Boca, Granny's passing, and the whole Kyle debacle.

"I guess that depends on what you're saying to Ben about me." Anger flies over me again at the thought, and I clench my fists. "How can you be doing the dirty with my brother when he's taking my home away from me?"

She puts her hands on my shoulders. "Maybe, just maybe, I can talk some sense into him—or *screw* some into him. I think this dress is pretty hot, right?"

She laughs and steps back to gesture to her slinky dress with its deep V-neck. Her favorite "fuck-me" heels are on—a pair of black Jimmy Choos we bought together on a girls' trip to Savannah. Her concerned gaze gauges my reactions.

"It's bros before hos then?"

She exhales, regret on her face, the corners of her mouth turning down. "It's not like that, Ash."

"It is like that. You chose him over me."

She sits on the bed, a defeated slump to her shoulders. "He kisses so damn good, and when he rubs my feet after a hard day of walking the dogs—"

"Oh, God. Just stop. I don't want to hear about you fornicating with my brother." I set my glass down on the vanity and apply more lipstick although I'm not really paying attention.

My hand shakes a little and I feel betrayed. Again.

Lulu sniffs and I turn to see that her eyes are glistening with tears.

Fuck me.

Lulu is a tough nut to crack. Hallmark movies won't do it, and even when she stubs her toe, she's invincible. The only time I ever recall her getting misty-eyed is when her beloved pet hamster broke his leg and passed.

"Don't cry, Lulu."

A tear falls down her face. "It's just... I'm really sorry to drop the Ben bomb on you after Jax. I'm a terrible person, an awful friend."

"No, you're not," I say softly.

She pats at her tears with a tissue I hand her. Her green eyes peer up at me. "You're so much more important than good sex. I'll ditch him altogether. I'll never fantasize about him again, I swear. I'll never even LOOK at him." Sadness passes over her features as she sends me a pleading look. "You and I are friends forever, like Thelma and Louise, but without the going over the cliff part."

THE RIGHT STUD

I sigh heavily, as the final tendrils of anger over Ben and Lulu fade. True, she is sleeping with the enemy but she's been dreaming of it since high school. And who knows? Maybe she can soften him.

"Don't stop seeing him. Not if you think there might be something real there. Ben's always been a good guy before. Maybe someone like you can bring him back to the light."

Hope flits across her face. "Really?"

I nod, feeling more firm and sure as I think about it. "I don't know what's going to happen with my house, but I do know that you will always be my friend and he'll always be my brother."

She nods up at me, and I reach down to give her a quick hug.

"Thank you. I had to tell you because I've felt so guilty. I'm going to do my best to talk to him about backing off."

I smirk ruefully. "Good luck with that. Ben seeing a pile of money is like a hummingbird seeing red."

We're distracted as Mrs. C waltzes in the room, Rufus sitting atop her shoulder.

"Ah, me so horny!" he squawks and flies off to roost on the curtain rod above my window.

I send him a glare. "Watch your language, buddy."

"Fuck off!" he cries.

I turn to Mrs. C to ask why she waltzed into my room with that bird and without even knocking when I see she's wearing an elaborately embroidered purple kaftan. She's taken off the turban and her graying blonde hair is styled in a fashionable up-do with soft curls framing her face. Pink lipstick adorns her lips, and her rouge is artfully applied to her cheekbones. I vaguely recall her mentioning going to the salon earlier this morning…

"Hello, ladies," she says airily. "I am beautiful, and I have arrived. What do you kids say? Oh yes, let's get this party started." She claps into the air.

"You're going with us?" Lulu sends me a questioning look.

I shrug. This is all news to me.

"We're going to a night club, Mrs. C." My voice is delicate. I don't want to offend her, but I also don't want her to have a heart attack. "It's going to be very loud with lots of flashing lights. Sweaty people will be everywhere, and some will smell worse than Rufus."

"A juke joint." She nods, rubbing her hands together. "It'll be like that time I took LSD at Burning Man."

I blink.

She continues. "And it's karaoke night at the Smoky Siren. I looked it up on the interwebs."

"It's the *internet*," I say.

"Potato, po-tah-toe." She waves her hand around and glides over to me, inspecting my dress. "Why, you look lovely, my dear."

"Thank you."

She nods, tapping her chin. "I've been trying to come up with a duet for us to sing all day, and I think I have it."

I laugh. "Are you sure you're up for all that?"

She arches her brow. "Please. I can out-party you any day of the week. You will sing with me, right? You can't turn me down, especially since I rarely go out." She thinks for a moment. "In fact, this is the first time I've been to a club since that night back in 1998 when Mr. C made love to me in a jazz bar down in New Orleans."

Oh.

"We got caught by the manager." She looks from me to Lulu. "Mr. C was going down on me. He was very talented with his tongue—"

"Well!" I clear my throat. "I can't wait to sing. What song did you have in mind?"

"How about 'I Will Survive'?" Lulu chimes in.

I huff out a laugh. "Goodness knows I need a girl-power song."

Mrs. C purses her lips. "I was thinking 'Like a Virgin' or 'Shake it Off.'" She does a little shimmy.

Lulu giggles.

"Fine. I'll sing whatever you want, Mrs. C, but first we have to get there, and since I'm buzzing from the bubbly already, let's get an Uber." I pull out my phone and order the car.

This is going to be one wild night.

Chapter 26

Jax

The New York skyline glows as the last rays of the sun glint, reflecting off the high-rises surrounding my apartment. I stand on my small balcony listening to the shouts and honks of the evening traffic on the Upper East Side.

It's a far cry from the beach in Palmetto, and as soon as my plane landed at JFK, a gnawing pit of regret settled in my stomach and took up residence. It hasn't left.

I take a sip of the scotch I poured earlier as my eyes drift along the horizon. I wonder what Ashton is doing. I picture her standing on the porch at The Conch, gazing out at the waves. Is she thinking about me right now? Is she missing me?

Don't be an idiot, Jax.

I left Palmetto because she threw me out. She fucking hates the sight of me.

Right.

I scrub at the scruff of evening shadow along my jawline—which reminds me I need to shave. It's been a few days, but I haven't felt like doing much since leaving South Carolina. If I had a therapist, they'd probably tell me I'm depressed.

Whatever. I have to get back to work and forget Ashton Hall.

I toss back another sip just as my doorbell rings. Stepping

into the den, I pass by the classic 1980s movie still running on my flatscreen TV. *How long has that been on repeat?*

A cardboard pizza box is on the floor with more than half a pizza inside, and an empty bottle of Jameson sits on the coffee table. The half-empty bottle I'm working on now is beside it. How much time has passed?

Pulling the door open I see Tara smiling, laptop in hand. I know she's here to see the work I did at The Conch. I told her I had a package to show the network. It's my dream, and everything about it has to be perfect. I need this gig. I need my time in South Carolina to mean something—besides breaking Ashton's heart.

Her eyes flare. "Holy cow. What happened to you? You look like shit."

Ashton happened.

"I went to bed late, I guess." I open the door wider as she breezes past.

"You look like you just woke up." Her gaze goes from my untucked dress shirt to my wrinkled slacks then back to my unshaven face. "Have you showered?"

I shrug. "Yes."

She waves toward my disheveled hair. "Are you sure?"

I push a wayward strand out of my face. "Scout's honor."

That gets me a wry smile. "You're no Boy Scout. Why aren't you all spiffed up and ready to head out for a night of womanizing?"

My lips curl downward. "That doesn't sound like me."

"It doesn't?" Tara's eyes bounce from the TV to me. "Are you watching *Against All Odds*?"

"Fuck no. It came on Skinamax. I'm waiting for the tits and ass." It's a lie. I've been wallowing in pizza, whiskey, and Phil

Collins. God help me. "I think I have a virus."

Tara's eyes narrow as she steps closer and catches my scruff in her hand. "What kind of virus?"

Tara's in her late forties, a whiz at public relations, and my go-to for negotiating sponsor deals for the show. She also acts like my surrogate big sister—as if I need another Bernice.

"Stomach bug or something."

At that she releases me and quickly wipes her hand on her pants. "Well, keep it to yourself."

I follow her into the office area I have set up off the kitchen, catching a glimpse of my reflection in the hall mirror. Shit, I *do* look like hell. My face is haggard, my eyes roadmaps from another sleepless night—and probably a bit too much liquor. It's the only way I can sleep since I got home. I can't stop thinking about those traces of tears on Ashton's cheeks. Hell, I even miss Mrs. C and Rufus.

When will this fucking *feeling* go away?

My teeth clench. I have to push these emotions aside and move on. I'm a heel, an asshole, a liar—*not* a hero, as Ashton properly noted. I pinch the bridge of my nose. If only I'd told her the whole story from the beginning…

Tara has settled into a chair across from my desk, an expectant look on her face. Right, she's here to go over the show—on a Friday—and I know she has places to be.

"Thanks for coming over," I say.

She shrugs. "No problem. Robert is making dinner for the kids, and I know you want to get this squared away as quickly as possible." She stops, a wrinkle appearing on her forehead. "Are you sure you're okay?"

I give her a terse nod. "Yes."

I will be… eventually.

Twisting my laptop around, I show her the edits I made. "Start here. Ashton was painting the molding and a seagull flew in. She threw a paintbrush at it."

Fuck, remembering it hurts. Tendrils of sadness curl through my chest.

Tara watches the segment, replaying it several times.

I'm not watching it. I can't look at it again, but I know what she's seeing. Ashton is wearing a pair of cutoff shorts and a bright yellow tank top as she stands on the ladder. Rufus is perched on the roof watching us, and Mrs. C is lurking in the window, her beady eyes not missing a thing.

Ashton explains to the camera the little touches her Granny made to the house, including painting mermaids everywhere, sometimes in secret locations. She's just found a small one she's never seen before. It's about the size of her hand on the trim around the ceiling. Her excitement is palpable as she paints around it, being careful to preserve the artwork.

Then the seagull swoops in and Ash squeals, throwing her paintbrush at it. She puts her hands on her hips and shakes her fist at the offending bird, belting out a few curses—which will have to be bleeped.

I recall how she looked back at me and started giggling. "Did you see that crazy bird? I wonder if it was the same one that chased Jean Claude into the ocean."

It was an incredible moment, a one-of-a-kind shot. The sun was behind her, touching the tips of her hair with golden light.

Tara is smiling. "That's a money shot. How on Earth did you keep from laughing?"

My hand involuntarily rubs my aching stomach. "It was hard, but I know a quality scene when I see it."

She nods, clearly excited as she speeds through me hammering boards on the porch. "I love it—all of it. It's like sassy Pioneer Woman meets the long-lost, blond Property Brother."

Her eyes dart across the screen, and I wait as she watches the package I spent most of the night editing together. For the life of me, I don't want to see it right now.

"Just *wow*. Celia is going to snatch this up. All of it is perfect for their Thursday night lineup, and you know they've been searching for something to replace *Fixer Upper*. I can see you doing an entire season on beach houses alone. The East Coast is covered in them!" Her lips purse as she thinks. "No one is doing that right now."

"I know." Everything she says is what I need to hear, but bitterness still eats at me.

She glances down at the laptop. "She's beautiful. The camera loves her."

"Yeah." My voice is flat.

The dreaded L-word.

Her eyes fly up to meet mine, as if something in my tone alerted her. "Did you tap that?"

I sigh as I stand to look out the window, drink in hand. I step over a pile of dirty clothes along the way. Fuck, this place is a mess, and I don't even care.

"Jax?" Her voice is concerned.

I toss a look at her. "What?"

"You can barely muster up any excitement about what I'm saying. What's going on with you?"

"I fucked everything up—*with her*."

"Come on. You're just out of sorts from being in Charleston. You always get this way when you visit home. Once we get this to Celia, everything will change—"

"You don't get it, Tara." Now I'm snapping at her when she

hasn't done a damn thing. Grabbing the reins, I lower my drink and adjust my tone. "I'm sorry. You should go. I'm sure your family is waiting on you."

She studies me, eyes squinted. "What happened between you and this girl?"

"Nothing."

"It doesn't look like nothing." She pauses. "Did you fall for her?"

My body freezes. *No.*

Fuck, if she's right, I hate it. It hurts and makes me want to yell at the top of my lungs.

"I'll get over it," I mutter as the music grows louder from my television. It's the sound of Phil Collins over the credits of the movie.

She marches over to the intrusive device and switches it off. "Tell me the truth. That's an order."

I rake both hands through my hair. Where to begin? "I told her why I left Charleston. I told her about my parents and fucking boarding school. I told her things I've never told anyone— not even you."

"Are you saying she's the only one who really knew you at all?" The tease in her tone snaps my eyes to hers.

Her lips fight a smile, and I feel simultaneously angry and foolish. I'm an idiot, and I decide to play along. "I just let her walk away from me."

"Oh my God. Shut the fuck up and go take a shower. We're sitting on a gold mine here, and you're wallowing like a lovesick teenager."

"I have a stomach bug."

"You're depressed. You're pining after this... really pretty girl." Tara's brow lifts as she nods toward my laptop, where the final shot of Ashton is frozen on the screen like an instrument of torture, a red-hot poker jammed in my aching chest. "She looks really sweet."

My voice is husky, broken. "She is." Again, I rub the pain in my midsection.

"You're in love with her."

"No." My answer is fast, sharp.

Crossing her arms over her chest, her expression morphs into disapproving parent. "Get your ass in that shower then get back to Palmetto and talk to her."

"She threw me out." Shaking my head, I can't believe I smile. "Literally. She threw my shit out the window."

"Sounds like she's in love with you, too."

With that, she's up and on the phone. Seconds later, I hear her ordering takeout from my favorite Italian place down the street.

She ends the call and gives me a serious look. "I've got your dinner handled. I want you to eat it and go to bed and get some real sleep." Her eyes go to the tumbler. "No more drinking."

"Okay." I sigh, rubbing my chest. I have no idea why I agree to what she's saying, but it just comes out.

She nods. "I'll handle everything with Celia. You are to get on a plane first thing in the morning and go back to Palmetto."

"I told you—"

She holds up a hand, cutting me off. "Go to that house and grovel."

"I already tried that." I walk over to sit on the couch. "She wasn't having it."

She walks over and pats me on the back. "Just go there. The plan will come."

"What is this, *Field of Dreams*?"

"It's better than the pussy-assed shit you've been listening to here. That song is about waiting for her to come back to you, and from what you've told me, it ain't happening."

Exhaling a laugh, I don't even try arguing. "You're saying it's 'Against All Odds'? What would you recommend instead?"

"The Finn Brothers." She pauses at the door and gives me a wink. "'Anything Can Happen.'"

Chapter 27

Ashton

Lying in my bed, the sun shines across my ceiling, and I stretch my arms over my head, remembering last night at the Smoky Siren. It all comes flooding back in a wave of triumph, and I cover my mouth as a satisfied smile lifts my cheeks.

Am I actually smiling? How long has it been since that happened? More importantly, how did this happen?

Well, I'll tell you…

We'd walked into that bar looking fierce, if I do say so myself. (I refuse to believe it's the prosecco remembering.) Even Mrs. C was bringing her A-game.

"The first thing we need to do is get the karaoke book," Mrs. C says, holding the door as I follow Lulu into the semi-crowded bar. "I read if you tip the DJ, they'll call your name faster."

"I'm not singing karaoke." Lulu slides a smooth lock of red hair behind her shoulder. "No amount of alcohol would make me sing in front of who knows who's listening."

"Oh, what are you worried about?" I grumble. "Ben's keeping the bed warm for you back at his place."

My best friend's jaw drops, but I shake my head. "Don't even bother—Mrs. C called it a week ago. She knows."

She looks from Mona to me, but I'm feeling my sparkling

wine. I push through the growing crowd to the bar and place my palm on the glossy wood.

The tall bartender looms over me, and I announce with gusto, "I'll have a martini! No ice, two olives."

His dark brow lowers. "Dirty?"

"You know it," I wink, no longer intimidated by his glower.

"Goodness," Mrs. C murmurs behind me. "Somebody's going to be barfing in the morning."

I watch as the man prepares the semi-complicated drink, and when he pours it into the tumbler, I hand it to the old lady behind me. "For you!"

Mrs. C's eyebrows shoot up as she takes it. "I haven't had one of these in, well, I can't even remember when."

A thin layer of ice floats on the top, and she takes a slow sip of the gin and vermouth concoction.

"Oh!" Her nose wrinkles as she passes it back to me. "I remember why it's been so long since I've had one of these— Christmas trees."

The music grows louder, a dance tune somewhere between Motown and David Guetta. I take a long sip of Christmas and toss my hands in the air. It's the first time I haven't felt like a boulder was squashing my heart in three days, and I want to dance.

We're out on the floor, bodies bouncing off us as we twist and sway to the music. Lulu is right beside me, twisting her hips with her eyes closed. Her hair swishes behind her in a silky curtain. Mrs. C is with us doing some sort of robot-style interpretive dance. The smoke machine goes off and lights streak through the bodies in thick bands. I close my eyes and forget everything as I'm swept up higher and higher...

Three songs later, we're at a high-top table, sweaty and

ordering more drinks. Mrs. C frowns, holding the plastic drink menu close to her face.

"I guess I read the website wrong. They don't have karaoke every night."

"Thank heaven for small mercies." Lulu holds her hair off her neck as she fans herself. "The last thing I want is to hear a bunch of drunks screaming off-key."

Mrs. C pats my arm. "We'll just have to come back tomorrow night."

I'm shaking my head as the waiter appears to take our orders. Lulu and I stick to prosecco while Mrs. C orders a margarita. "And put a jalapeño in it!"

That makes me smile. I reach out to cover the old woman's forearm with my hand, giving it a squeeze. A Bruno Mars song blasts over the loudspeakers, and Lulu slides out of her chair, doing a little hip-twisty move.

I'm about to join her when the door opens, and the air whooshes out of my lungs. I sit quickly, ducking to take a sip of my fresh drink as Monica struts inside wearing a red wrap dress with Kyle following behind her. His head is lowered, and he reminds me of Lulu's Chihuahua the day the skunks got spooked. Cowed.

"Well, look what the cat dragged in." My best friend speaks loud enough for them to hear, and I cringe when Monica turns to face us.

"Lulu," I hiss. The last thing I want is a showdown on the night I'm getting back on my feet.

Too late. Monica straightens her shoulders and marches her bony ass right to the high top table beside us. Kyle's eyes meet mine, and his brow lifts slightly. He almost looks happy to see me. What a bastard. *Monica not treating you right, dear?*

I don't have time for his bullshit.

"If your grandmother was here…" Mrs. C lifts the jalapeño out of her drink and starts to bite it. Then she seems to think better of it and lowers it into the icy, lime-green mixture instead.

Only… Her words do something to my insides. I remember the day at The Silver Spoon and how Monica had tried to make me feel like a slut for taking in boarders at The Conch. I remember what a yellow-bellied coward she was when Jax put her in her place, and I know all of her arrogance is just an act.

The music switches to a slow song. It's quieter, and several couples start to dance all hugged up and swaying. I wonder if Kyle will dance with Monica, and I'm gratified to realize I don't give a shit at all.

They don't go to the dance floor. They stand at that table, and Monica glares at me, wrinkling her nose. "You know Kyle," she says in a loud voice. "I've been thinking of doing some tarot readings of my own."

"What?" He frowns at her, clearly confused.

"I was just telling Rayleen it wouldn't be long before Ashton lost her house. I even predicted she'd be alone again."

My jaw clenches, and I weigh the pros and cons of fighting with words versus throwing my drink in her face. Lulu interrupts my violent plotting.

"Hey, Ash," she says, equally loudly while nodding toward Monica. "Don't you have a dress just like that one?"

Blinking the hot anger out of my eyes, I study the red wrap dress with tiny white polka dots and a ruffle around the hem. It's the very dress I had on at lunch that day.

"Well, I'll be a—"

"I wouldn't be surprised if she starts trolling home improvement shows next, pitching her bony butt as a sidekick. Kyle had better watch his back."

Monica's eyes and mouth are round as saucers. She flounces around the table to stand beside my ex. "Don't listen to her, Kyle. As if I care about anything she does."

No more acting like we're not talking to each other. I slide off my stool and face my nemesis head-on.

"I think you do." My voice is loud and strong. "I think you do everything you can to copy me. Why is that, Monica? Is original thought really so hard for you?"

Lulu steps around beside me, placing her hand on her hip. "They say imitation is the sincerest form of flattery."

"It's the sincerest form of stupidity if you ask me." My eyes are flashing fire, and strength is surging through my chest. I step to Monica, and she takes a step away, toward Kyle. "Maybe one day you'll stop being a lying, fiancé-stealing, backstabbing copy cat and just be yourself. Unless... that *is* yourself." I tilt my head and turn to Lulu. "Heck, I think I figured it out. That's all she is."

"You wish that's all I am," Monica snaps while my back is turned.

When I turn around, she cowers behind Kyle again. I'm undeterred. "I'm only going to say this once." Our eyes meet, and she's blinking fast. "Stay out of my way. I'm done with your bullshit."

Kyle starts to defend her, but I slice him a new one with my gaze as well. He shrinks back, and I feel good. Calm and good. And suddenly tired, as if a weight has been lifted.

I put my glass on the table. "Let's go, girls. This place has gotten too skanky for my taste."

With that I walk calmly to the exit. I'm ready to head back to The Conch.

"That's what I call a BURN!" Mrs. C calls to them, following behind me. "Did you hear what she said? Need me to spell it out for you? Stay out of Bad-Ash's way."

She's taunting, and I roll my eyes, grinning as I push through the door into the night air. Lulu is right behind me, saying goodnight to us before she heads to my brother's. Mrs. C and I wait for the Uber.

When we got back to The Conch, we had some decaf and shared a little celebratory cake before hitting the feathers.

This morning, I'm lying in bed, luxuriating in the waves of power moving through me. I feel good. I feel at ease.

Yet, I don't feel happy. Not really.

Pushing the blankets aside, I walk to the bathroom and splash water on my face. I lift the towel and touch it to my cheeks, thinking about the reasons everything is good, why I feel like I've grown and changed. Why something is still missing.

I've said what I needed to say to the people who deserve to hear it. I've taken control back, but as those days were passing, while I was getting stronger, I was also falling in love.

I really did, and it felt so true and real.

Mrs. C is in the kitchen when I enter wearing a bright green sundress. She's in her blue and yellow pajamaralls with a red handkerchief tied around her head, and she's pouring a mug of coffee. Rufus is on the curio, bobbing his head to George Harrison's "My Sweet Lord" playing softly on the radio.

"You're up early." I pass behind Mrs. C to get a mug of my own. "Didn't you sleep well?"

"I woke up in the mood to do some fishing."

"Oh?"

She smiles. "Last night got me thinking about all the fish in the sea, which then got me thinking about how Mr. C and I used to love to fry up some fresh perch with red and yellow bell peppers, ground paprika, a little onion and garlic."

"So no breakfast for you?"

She puts her cup on the counter and pats my arm. "I'll catch us something good to eat for lunch instead." With a wave, Rufus descends to her shoulder, and they head out the side door.

I watch as she scoops up a cane pole and a small pail of dirt, and I realize she's been up a while if she had time to dig for grubs. Then I wonder where in the world she managed to find grubs around here with all the sand.

I shake my head as I walk over to the cabinet. Taking down my pale green mixing bowl, I pull out the dry ingredients. I step to the refrigerator and take out milk and eggs and a small basket of blueberries.

My feet are bare, and as I start to fold the ingredients together, the ache expands in my chest. As proud as I am for how much I've changed, for standing up to Monica and walking out with my head high, it's impossible to forget all the things that happened on the journey. I remember the days Jax and I spent together, starting with the kiss in that bar.

But he lied to you, Ashton. My head refuses to budge on this, and I know it's right.

Still, I remember him walking around the house, studying it so intently that first day. I remember him saying he'd help me, and how impossibly happy I'd been. Why would he do all that work if he was only in it for the money?

To get in your pants, you naïve child. Once again, my brain rises up to chastise me.

But, oh, man, how amazing was it when he finally *did* get into my pants? I squeeze my thighs together as I turn the thickening batter with my wooden spoon. Reaching for the muffin pan, I give it a quick spritz with cooking oil before dropping portions into each of the cups.

He sat on the floor with me in my closet, listening to me talk about the mural Granny painted. He rescued JC from drowning. He even crawled under that house to get rid of the skunk family.

After that, my memories become a whirlwind of heat and lust and laughter and playfulness. We sat on the beach and talked and talked. We lay in his bed and talked and talked. We watched movies. We held hands. He defended me against Monica when I was still finding my feet. He introduced me to his family.

We were just so comfortable in each other's arms.

What did he say that last day? I slide the pan into the hot oven as I try to remember...

"I never let him explain," I say to myself, my eyes drifting to the window.

"Is it too late to try again?" I jump a foot in the air at the low male voice before spinning around to face him.

My heart thuds, and Jax stands on the other side of the screen door, looking at me with so much intensity in his blue eyes.

Chapter 28

Is it possible Jax looks better than ever? He's only wearing jeans and a light-blue oxford, but his eyes glow from beneath his lowered brow.

"Sorry." His expression is concerned. "I didn't mean to scare you."

Clearing my throat, I manage to speak. "What are you doing here?"

His chin drops, and he lifts the leather case he's holding. "My producer loved the work we did. I put together a demo, and she's pitching it to HGTV. We're pretty confident they're going to go for it."

Blinking quickly, I try to understand what he's saying. "But... did you tell them my brother wants to sell? I could lose the house?"

It still provokes a burning at the base of my throat when I say the words. My brother is giving me acid reflux.

"If the show gets picked up, it'll change everything." He's studying me so intently, I have to break his gaze.

Glancing down, I slide my hands over the skirt of my cotton dress. A dark, wavy lock falls over my eye, and I remember I'm standing on the wooden floors in my bare feet.

I'd never thought about how much I run around here bare-foot until Jax noticed. Lifting my chin, I catch his eyes still on me, only now they look... hungry. It makes my skin hot.

"How would everything change?" My voice is suddenly thick.

"It would mean a lot of money flowing into the project. It would mean free restorations for the house, free publicity if you wanted to run it as a B&B." He pauses, allowing his eyes to drift down my body to my feet and up again. It's like a caress. "If this works out the way I want it to, the way I've wanted it to since the first day I was here, it could take things to a whole new level."

He's saying everything I hoped might happen when I emailed him months ago, inviting him to come for a visit. Only... "What do you want to happen?"

The blue in his eyes seems to darken, and I flush from head to toe.

"I want to save this house. I want you on the show." He clears his throat and lifts the leather portfolio he's holding. "You're a natural in front of the camera, Ash. Tara, my producer, and I agree you'd be a great addition, if that's some-thing you'd be interested in doing. It doesn't have to be full-time —"

Heat simmers in my chest with every word he speaks.

Wait. *He wants me on his show?*

"You mean I'd be like Jeffrey on *The Barefoot Contessa*?" Confusion lines his brow, and I hastily explain. "Jeffrey is her husband. She's the main one on the show all the time, but he'll pop in and sample something she's made or she'll say she's cooking this for Jeffrey..."

I'm rambling, but understanding dawns across his face. "It's a cooking show?"

"You've never heard of *The Barefoot Contessa*?"

"Can I come inside?"

Electricity flashes through me at his tone, and I swallow before wiping my sweaty palm over my middle.

"I guess so." Stepping forward, I reach for the door, but he's already pulling it open.

I take a step back, and his presence absolutely fills my kitchen. Another step back, and my butt hits the counter, my elbow slides a mug out of the way.

"Would you like some coffee? I'm making muffins…"

"They smell delicious." He steps closer, and my stomach tightens. My head feels hot, and there's no escaping him.

Blinking fast, I search for anything to say. "So you were saying you want me to be on your show?"

He places both hands on the counter, caging me in his arms. "The camera loves you."

"The camera?" I lift my chin, and our lips are a breath apart.

"Mm-hm." His warm breath skates over my cheek, and his eyes capture mine.

So many memories swirl in our gaze, but a sliver of resistance remains in my brain. "I'm still mad… about before."

He nods, moving his face as if he's inhaling my scent. "I should have told you everything." Warm eyes hold mine. "I knew if I told Ben no, he'd find someone else to sell the place. I didn't want anyone else coming in here. I wanted to be the one to save it. I wanted to be your hero."

"You barely even knew me."

"When I kissed you in that bar, I didn't know you at all." His face seems to dip lower. Or maybe my chin lifts higher.

"I'm just another goat in the ocean to you."

THE RIGHT STUD

A laugh rumbles deep in his throat as his hands move closer, capturing me in a full-on embrace. "You're much softer than Jean Claude." Dipping his head to my ear, he inhales lightly. "You smell better, too."

My hands slide up his arms to his shoulders. "So I'm a kitten in a tree?"

"No." He lifts his head so our eyes can meet, and his expression turns serious. "You're an amazing woman. You're smart and stubborn and loyal, and you're a natural at doing my job. I'm sorry I didn't tell you everything. I never wanted to hurt you."

"Don't ever do it again."

"I promise I won't." His nose touches mine. "Can I kiss you now?"

My eyes flicker to his full lips, and I stretch up to meet them. Soft and warm, they push mine apart, and his tongue sweeps inside, curling with mine and lighting me up like a firecracker.

A little noise escapes from my throat, and the temperature in the kitchen skyrockets. His hands are on my hips, fingers curling as he gathers my skirt higher. I'm throbbing with need, clutching his face in my hands, scratching my fingers through his light beard. I'm ready to climb him like a tree, when—

"The muffins are burning!" Mrs. C flies through the screen door with Rufus right behind her screeching.

"Fucking teenagers!" The bird lands on the curio, shifting from foot to foot as he settles in his spot.

We break apart quickly, and I grab a hot pad to retrieve the baked goods from the oven. Mrs. C is beside me holding long silver tongs in one hand and wearing an oven mitt on the other.

"Save the lovemaking for later. Don't burn my breakfast!"

"You said you didn't want any breakfast," I fuss, holding the pan upside down and giving it a shake.

The slightly over-browned muffins drop into the basket as Mrs. C leans over to inspect them, turning them quickly with the tongs.

"I was halfway to the creek when I saw Studly here coming up the lane. Decided to double back and make sure you didn't need any help."

Jax's voice is a sly tease. "You wanted to spy on us is more like it."

"I did not!" The old woman draws up, crossing her arms over her chest. She only holds the pose a moment before breaking down with a wink. "That was some damn fine apologizing, though. Reminds me of the time Mr. C tried putting a Carolina Reaper on my nachos. That's the hottest pepper in the world, you know, grown right here in our home state of South Carolina. Well, that was the final straw. I packed up, ready to drive to Mama's when he promised never to pull a stunt like that again."

I can't resist another second. "Mrs. C, why was Mr. C always plying you with hot peppers?"

She shrugs. "He loved 'em. Wanted me to love 'em too, I guess. That's kind of how it is, I suppose. When you love someone, you want to share everything you love with them." Her eyes go to Jax, traveling from his waist to his chiseled face. "Kind of like you're doing with that construction show you're working on, right Studly?"

"I don't know." Jax clears his throat and shifts from one foot to the other. "We haven't really gotten that far into the conversation—"

"Then it sounds like I need to clear out of here! Come on, Rufus! These two have some confessing to do." She waves her arm, and the bird swoops down to land on her shoulder before they both head farther into the house.

A few moments later, we hear her door close loudly. I shake my head, exhaling a laugh. "That woman. If she didn't remind me so much of my granny, I don't know what I'd do."

Jax frowns. "Your granny was like that?"

"No!" My nose wrinkles. "Granny just loved that old bat. Having her around makes me remember all the times we would laugh and roll our eyes. I wasn't very big, but it was like we had an inside secret being amused by her. It made me feel like a grown-up."

Jax steps closer and pulls me into his arms again. "It sounds like you had the best kind of relationship with her." I nod, tracing my finger around the small, pearl-white button on the front of his oxford as he inhales deeply. "She's right, you know?"

"How's that?"

"I do have a confession to make." His expression is something I've never seen on him. *Is Jax Roland worried?*

My chest squeezes, and he says it, slightly breathless. "I think I love you, Ashton Hall."

An irresistible smile shoots across my face following the thrill racing from my feet to my cheeks. "You think?" My voice goes high.

That makes him laugh. He drops his head back and lets out an exaggerated sigh. "Okay, I *know* I love you." Catching my eyes again, his are sparkling as he kisses my nose. "These past few days were torture. I felt like such an ass breaking your heart. Working on that package nearly killed me."

"This is all good to hear." I'm grinning from ear to ear as I rise on my toes to kiss his lips. "Because I think I love you, too."

"That does it." He bends down and swoops me into his arms Cinderella-style, and I let out a shriek. "I'm taking you to bed."

"Yes, please!" I'm reaching to give him another kiss, when

—

"Ashton?" My brother's loud voice shouts across the porch. *Jeez Louise!*

Lulu is right behind him. "She's probably in the kitchen. Here."

I push on Jax's shoulder, and my feet just touch the floor when the two of them come barging inside. I cross my arms and cock my hip, preparing for battle.

"Oh, here you are." Ben only casts me a glance before his eyes land on Jax. "What are you doing here?"

"That's none of your business," I answer quickly. "What are *you* doing here?"

"You don't have to be such a pill, Ashton. Lulu convinced me to come over here and talk to you."

My brother's success at running his own law firm has slowly turned him into a very *my way or the highway* type of guy. I know having to acquiesce to me is a new feeling for him.

I nod at my bestie. "So you two are out of the closet now?"

"We're straight," Ben says with an impatient sigh. "It's not the same metaphor."

"I think that metaphor can be used for any type of secret relationship... never mind. What do you want to talk to me about?"

He inhales slowly, pinching the bridge of his nose. "Lulu says you have something to show me."

Confusion lines my brow, and my eyes fly to my bestie's.

"Speaking of closets." Her chin rises and she nods toward the upstairs. "It's *in* your closet."

Jax's phone starts to ring, and he gives my arm a squeeze. "Be right back."

He takes the call into the living room, and I realize what

Lulu is saying. Not convinced it will work, I motion for my brother to follow me, and to my surprise, he does, up the stairs and down the hall to my room.

"Lavender," my brother says as we enter, his voice uncharacteristically gentle. "It still smells like Granny in here."

"I cleaned out all her clothes." Opening the closet door, I pull the string for the light, illuminating the mermaid mural on the wall. *The girl who has everything…*

Except the one woman she'd give anything to have back.

"What is this?" Ben's voice is hushed.

"You probably don't remember the summer I watched *The Little Mermaid* nonstop."

"Are you kidding me?" The way he says it, laughter cracking in his throat, he sounds seventeen again. "I still have every song in that movie memorized thanks to you. You wouldn't turn it off."

"It was the same summer she took that art class. The year she met Mrs. C. She made this for me. She told me it would always be my mermaid."

I can still see her eyes wrinkle with her smile as she said it, and I cross my arms over the ache in my chest.

I had no idea at the time how many mermaids she'd hidden around this old house. Now I wonder if there's a little merman hidden somewhere for my brother.

"Why didn't I know about this?" His speaks just above a whisper.

My eyes are hot, and I don't try to answer. I only shrug.

A strong arm goes around my shoulders, and my brother pulls me into his chest. It's the first time he's been this open since our long argument began.

"I didn't know." He's quiet a moment, and I feel myself

relax listening to his breath swirling in and out. "I'm sorry I didn't take into account how deep your feelings were when it comes to this place."

My arms relax and I nod. "Apology accepted."

He steps back. His eyes are warm, but his mouth is a straight line. "I still think selling is the right thing. You can't argue with the facts, Ashton—"

Jax's loud laughter interrupts us, and I give my brother a frown before stepping out of the closet and hurrying down the hall. Jax dashes into the foyer from the living room, and we meet each other at the bottom of the stairs.

"They love it!" he shouts, catching me around the waist, lifting me off my feet, and spinning me around.

Mrs. C bursts into the room, Rufus on her shoulder squawking.

My heart is racing. My hands are on Jax's shoulders, and my body is pressed against his firm chest. "Was that Tara? What did she say?"

"HGTV ordered five episodes for the fall. We got an on-air commitment, and if it plays well with audiences, they'll give us a full season."

"A full season!" My voice is a squeal, and I hug his head. "That's amazing! I'm so happy for you!"

"Happy for *us*. They want you as well. They loved you."

"Me?" It's difficult to breathe thinking about what he's saying. "I'm your Jeffrey?"

"You're my Jeffrey, and I haven't even tell you the best part."

"It gets better?"

Ben cuts through the commotion, ducking as he passes Rufus. "What is this about? What's going on here?"

Jax lowers to me to my feet and answers him. "*The Right Stud* just got picked up by HGTV." Turning to me again, he cups my cheek. "They're providing a budget that will more than cover all the renovations on your list with enough left over to beat any kind of profit you'd make from a sale."

I literally can't breathe. "What are you saying?" My hands tremble as I cover my mouth with my fingers, my eyes growing hotter.

Jax turns to my brother. "I'm saying Ashton wins. There's no way a buyer can top what the studio is putting down, combined with the national publicity, the sponsorships, endorsements, and the flood of visitors—should Ash decide she wants to run this place as a bed and breakfast."

I win.

The words wash through me like a tidal wave, sweeping all the anxiety and sorrow out, leaving security, adventure, and a confession of love in its wake.

My brother's brow lifts. "They sent you a contract I can look over? My sister is new to this business, and I want to make sure her interests are protected."

Jax wraps his arm around my shoulder, pulling me tight into his side. "Don't worry. We've got time to work out the details. I've got Ashton's best interests in mind."

"Still, I want to be sure…"

My brother continues talking, but Jax drags me out the screen door onto the porch away from the crowded house. We stop at the corner where we worked, where the sun shines on new wood and fresh paint.

Waves crash on the shore down to my right, but I'm lost in the gaze of the man I love—a man I was not looking for and never dreamed I'd get to know so well. His hands are on my cheeks, and our noses are almost touching.

He smiles, white teeth and that completely unfair dimple showing, as he asks me softly, "Am I your hero now?"

"You're more than my hero." I rise on my toes to capture his full lips. "You're The Right Stud who completely changed my life."

"I intend to keep on changing it."

"How so?"

His low chuckle sends a thrill through my insides. "You'll just have to stay tuned to find out."

Our mouths meld together in a long kiss, one of mended pasts and broken dreams transformed into something shining and new.

Jax's arms go around my waist, and I smile up at the tiny mermaid my grandmother painted, hidden in the eaves. *We saved it, Granny.*

Ahead of us now is the bright future we're building together.

Epilogue

Jax

Five years later

"Do you think we should make her stop?" I murmur to Ashton as I watch our blonde little girl chase Jean Claude van Ram across the beach. It's the middle of June, and the sun shines down on the water, catching the tips of the crashing waves and making them sparkle. It's a damn near perfect day. I let out a sigh of contentment.

"Mama, Dada, watch me!" Bre giggles as she dashes past us again, her little toddler feet snapping on the heels of JC who keeps turning his head back to look at her. Periodically, he'll slow down to let her catch up then he'll snort something in his goat language and take off again.

I chuckle and answer my own question. "Nah, I think he's okay with it. The old goat likes it."

Ashton, who is nearly asleep as I keep watch on the pair, peeks out from under her wide-brimmed straw sunhat. We're both settled in lounge chairs underneath a big blue umbrella.

Half an hour earlier, we ran all over the beach and played in the waves with Bre, searching for sand dollars and starfish.

We walked down here after she and Bre cooked me Father's Day breakfast, a frittata and blueberry muffins, just like the ones she made the morning I showed up at The Conch and met her—for the second time.

My eyes drift over Ashton's oval face, drinking in the smooth skin, kind hazel eyes, and dark hair she's braided and curled around her head. We've haven't been apart a single day since the moment I came back to Palmetto and told her I loved her. Everything has turned out to be more than I ever could have even dreamed.

I think back over the past five years. We had a short engagement and a small wedding right here on the beach within a year of meeting. I resigned from my job with Pearson and the show made it possible for Ashton to make all the upgrades to The Conch she'd always wanted but never had the money to do. New wide-plank flooring, an upgraded kitchen, and an additional bathroom for guests were just some of the improvements.

The Right Stud soared to the top of the rankings, turning Ashton and me into household names. She and I film it together, and like Tara said, she's a natural in front of the camera. The viewers love her genuine smile and southern sass. Combine that with my good looks and charm, and well, it's a hit.

We travel and shoot the show in the fall and spring and spend summers and winters here at The Conch. Lulu manages the day-to-day of the B&B, and even Ben stops by to help her on the weekends. Or maybe he just spends the night. I don't ask.

I glance back at Ashton, my heart full. It's an idyllic life, and to think I never imagined I could have it. My new family is the best thing I never knew I needed.

Ashton gives the pair running across the beach a little smirk. Wearing a red bikini that contrasts beautifully with her tanned skin and dark hair, she's gorgeous. "If Lulu didn't want him to get chased, she shouldn't have left him here with us to babysit."

Impulsively, I lean over and kiss her lightly on the lips.

She peers up at me through her thick lashes. "Are you happy? Are you having a good Father's Day?"

I tug her nape closer to me as our bodies turn toward each other on our lounge chairs. "More than happy. Ecstatic. I couldn't ask for anything else."

Her lips curve up in a beautiful smile. "I have a surprise for you. Pretty soon, she'll have a little brother or sister to boss around."

I suck in a sharp breath at the tidal wave of love that overwhelms me. My heart swells. My body hums.

"Are you sure? We've been trying for the past year…"

She nods. "I just found out last week." She bites her lip and gives me a sheepish smile. "It's been hard to keep it from you, but I wanted today to be special. I'm eight weeks."

Her hand curls protectively around her stomach.

Emotion clogs my throat as I shake my head. "I love you, Ash. So much, babe."

"I love you too." Her voice is soft and full of the same emotion I have in my heart.

I grin, remembering how we met. "I'm thankful every day that you emailed my show and I had the good sense to show up in your kitchen. Fate knew what she was doing when she brought us together—even if the road was a little bumpy getting here."

She laughs. "I still giggle when I think back to you dashing into the ocean to save JC."

I waggle my brows. "I impressed you with my goat-saving skills, right?"

She laughs. "Um, it was definitely those six pack abs you were sporting. That goat is a nuisance."

I grin. "Wanna head up to the room? I'll let you touch my

abs—and other parts—all you want."

Our daughter squeals with laughter and we both look over to see that she has the goat by the horns and is attempting to ride him like a horse.

Ashton stands up, dusting stray bits of sand from her legs. "Looks like we might need to rescue that animal from our precious three-year-old."

I grin and take her hand as we walk toward them. Off in the distance, I see Mrs. C and Rufus standing on the porch watching us. She waves, and we both wave back.

Contentment curls around me. *I'm home,* I think. *I'm exactly where I want to be*. Forever.

Ashton sighs gently, giving my hand a squeeze, and I know it's her way of telling me she feels the same.

—

Thank you for reading THE RIGHT STUD!
We hope you love Ashton and Jax's story as much as we do.

Want to read MORE Tia-Ilsa books in Kindle Unlimited?

Check out our sexy "enemies to lovers" romantic comedy THE LAST GUY.

Keep turning for an Exclusive Sneak Peek…

Chapter 1

Rebecca

Scratchy pink tulle hits me square in the face, and I jerk away as a shrieking tornado of blonde curls bolts past me. I am in hell, more specifically *pageant* hell, the deepest and darkest level.

"Petal Boo Bishop! PETAL BOO BISHOP!" A large woman stomps after the child, shoving me as I dodge to avoid being tackled. "Get back here and put your tutu on this minute!"

My camera-guy Kevin snorts as I regain my footing. He gets a brief, snappy glare. Let him try interviewing tiny humans in the middle of chaos.

Clearing my throat, I smile and hold the mic down to the four-foot beauty queen I'd been addressing before the interruption. "And what will you do if you win Miss Planetary Princess, Kaitlyn?"

She pushes her helmet of golden-brown hair away from her face. It's bigger than her head and strong enough to withstand any climatological distress. My hair, by contrast, is completely wilted and flat in the Houston humidity that blasts through the room every time a door opens.

"First, I wanna eat chicken nuggets then pizza with pineapple and a Coke—oh, and some taco bells. I haven't had a taco since I was three years old. Mama says tacos are bad for business."

Mama gives Kaitlyn a warning look.

"That sounds like my kind of fun!" I laugh, giving her a fist bump and then winking at the camera. The wink is my trademark, along with my pencil skirts.

Kaitlyn's mama charges me, putting her hand on the mic alongside mine and giving it a tug. I tug back—while pretending I'm not—as I smile through clenched teeth. I refuse to let go, and she hunches in front of me to speak.

"After we win here, we're heading to Little Miss Galaxy at the San Francisco Zoo," she states. "We'll go straight to catwalk training and poise. The girls in Little Miss Galaxy come from all over the country, you know. Their bodies are streamlined and toned—no baby fat. We're on a healthy but strict diet."

I blink in horror as I absorb her speech. *Think about the anchor job, Rebecca. Smile.* "Wow. That seems rigorous for a five-year-old."

Mama rakes her eyes over me. "I'm sure you wouldn't know anything about it."

I jerk the mic away, ignoring her body shaming. "Kaitlyn, how do *you* feel about being Miss Galaxy?"

"*Little* Miss Galaxy," her mother corrects.

Huge brown eyes gaze up at me. "I'll be Princess Leia!"

Mama bursts out laughing. "With that honey-bun hair! You are *not* Princess Leia. Except for maybe those chubby cheeks, but we're working on that."

The child's eyes land on her shoes, and I swallow the knot of anger in my throat. I might be a hard-boiled newswoman, but I'm fighting a deep desire to steal this little cutie and give her a normal childhood—tacos and all.

Looking straight into Kevin's lens, I do the wrap. "There

you have it, folks. Miss Planetary Princess is just the latest preschool pageant feeding into the Miss USA circuit. Catch all the taco-worthy drama tomorrow night at eight, right here at the Houston Expo Center. I'm Rebecca Fieldstone, KHOT News."

I hold the smile a beat longer until Kevin gives me the signal. "We're clear."

He lowers the camera, and my shoulders drop. This assignment is soul sucking.

I need to get back to the station and edit the story, but I can't help sneaking a last look at Kaitlyn. Her shoulders are also slumped, and her mom steers her in the direction of the Channel 8 news team set up in the corner across from us. I hope she gets a taco soon.

"You ready?" I tuck the mic under my arm and pick up my bag.

"Miss? Excuse me, miss?" The large woman who had almost knocked me down earlier touches my shoulder.

I don't stop walking.

The woman keeps my pace, breathing heavily as she jogs. "Sorry about earlier, but you haven't talked to Petal Boo. We'd really like to have her on camera for her résumé."

Not another one, I groan inwardly. "I'm sorry. I can't guarantee what goes on air—"

The lady shoots out a hand and grips my arm, stopping me. "Oh, you'll want to talk to Petal. She's not like the rest."

My eyebrow arches, and she releases me. Still, her face is pleading. "Just take a look. Please?"

Something about her gives me pause. Maybe it's the sweat lining her brow—I can totally relate. As per usual, it's a steamy late-September day in southeast Texas, and I left my blotting papers back in the news van. I'm sure my face looks like a red

Solo cup right now.

Giving Kevin a quick nod, we follow her. My mic is out, the light goes on, and Kevin points the camera at a fluffy little girl in a white-blonde wig styled with long ringlets around her oval face.

"Hi, there," I say with a smile. "What's your name?"

She throws back her shoulder and tilts her chin. "My name is Petal Boo Bishop, and I'm from Meridian, Mississippi!" She's practically shouting in her clipped country accent, but her execution is polished. "I got started in the pageant circuit after I won the Beautiful Child competition. You've probably heard of the Beautiful Child pageant. It's famous."

"I'm afraid I haven't—"

"From *To Kill a Mockingbird*? You haven't read *To Kill a Mockingbird*?" Her tone is astonished disapproval.

The camera trembles with Kevin's suppressed laughter, and I smile, knowing good footage when I see it. I bend down to her level, sucking in my gut. From this angle, it's more of a challenge to hide the extra few pounds I've picked up these last couple months.

"It's been a while," I say, and she charges on.

"It's been voted one of the greatest novels of all time. It concerns the evils of racism."

"You're a smart girl, Petal. How old were you when you won Beautiful Child?"

Her face snaps to the camera. "I was four years old when I won my first contest. After that my mama said I could win a bunch of money in pageants, so we hit the road. We've been to Atlanta, Tampa, Nashville, Baton Rouge, and now we're here in the great state of Texas to claim Miss Planetary Princess." Her arm goes straight up, victory style, and she says it all without even pausing for breath.

"Okay, then." I stand, taking the pressure off my back. "Good luck to you, Petal."

"Thank you, Miss Fieldstone."

This kid knows my name? "How old are you now?"

"Seven and a half. I'm right slap in the middle of the playing field." She does a little hip-cock—as much as possible in her fluffy pink dress. "This is gonna be my year, just you wait and see. I'm gonna take home the tiara."

Her mother rocks back on her heels, arms crossed, beaming with pride.

"In that case, I'll be watching for you, as will Houston tonight at six and ten. Do you have a special message for our Channel 5 viewers?"

"You bet your butt I do." She looks into the camera. "People of Texas and the world, don't settle. You deserve the best, just like me. Work as hard as you can and have some fun too." She gives the camera a thumbs-up. "Y'all take care now!"

I watch her prance off, tutu flouncing with every step, and I confess, I'm a little envious of her confidence. That's *exactly* the kind of attitude I need when it comes to getting the weekend anchor position. It's been on my radar ever since Maryanne announced she isn't coming back from maternity leave. She wants to start a family, and her decision is my chance to get off this underpaying, exhausting reporter's beat. *Please, God,* I pray silently. *I need that anchor job.*

Back in the van, I flip down the visor and lean forward to check my appearance as Kevin races us to the studio. We've got exactly forty-five minutes to get this package together for the six o'clock news.

"My nose looks like an oil slick, and I've got mascara specks under my eyes." *Shit!* My gaze cuts to Kevin. "Why didn't you say something?"

Kevin takes a loud slurp from his Big Gulp. With frizzy brown hair and two-inch thick glasses, he's the consummate tech geek, wrinkled shirt and all. "I didn't notice. Petal was more interesting."

I groan and dig through my oversized purse, pulling out a small compact of pressed powder to blot my face. *Why didn't I check the mirror before that stupid segment?*

Marv, our overbearing news director, could catch a speck of pepper in your back teeth. I'm dead. Glancing out the window, I wonder if we could possibly get back and do a re-shoot... Who am I kidding? No telling where Petal Boo is now, and depending on the downtown traffic, we barely have time to get to the station.

"You look fine, Becks." Kevin takes another slurp. "You're always too hard on your appearance."

I glare at him, and he shrugs, keeping his eyes on the road. *Fine* doesn't cut it these days. You have to be young and pretty much perfect to land an anchor gig. They're the top-paying, most visible spots in the broadcast-news food chain.

We're finally at the studio, and I dash to the editing booth to pick the video clips and put the story together. Most of Kaitlyn's interview ends up on the cutting-room floor in favor of scene-stealer Petal Boo. It's sad, but I can't help grinning as I realize Petal might be the one bright spot of my week. Even though I look like a disheveled mess standing next to the tiny, spray-tanned beauty queen, I don't mind so much. She's got loads of personality, and she's definitely one to watch.

I record my voice-over and layer it on top of B-roll of little girls teasing hair the size of Texas and twirling around in thousand-dollar sequined evening gowns, bedazzled cowgirl boots, and glittering one-piece swimsuits. The entire package is ready to go as the Channel 5 theme music begins.

"Becks! I need that story now!" Vicky, our executive producer, waves at me from the end of the short hall where the editing booths are located.

I punch *Save* and give her the thumbs-up. "It's on the server ready to roll!"

Leaning back in my chair, I think about the old days when a kid with a cart full of tapes would run the stories to the control room. It's so much easier now that digital has replaced film.

Standing, I don't even bother tucking my white blouse into my skirt. Hell, it's too tight anyway. My shoes are in my hand, and I collect my jacket and purse ready to call it a day. I've been at the station since nine, just in time to catch the morning show wrap up before heading out on my assignment. I'll stop by my desk and check my emails before I leave.

Of course, my path takes me right past the sports den, a newly renovated space consisting of desks and computers arranged in the shape of an octagon, *like an MMA fighting arena.* I don't even try to suppress my eye roll. Still... the one thing that stops them rolling is our new sports director.

With wavy dark hair and steel-blue eyes, Cade Hill has been here less than three months, and already he's revamped the entire department into a slick, SportsCenter-style man-paradise.

He's an ex-NFL superstar, son of a millionaire, and infuriating as hell. After retiring from the Atlanta Falcons, where he was the starting quarterback before blowing out his knee, he came here and was immediately put in charge of sports. He has zero experience, and he thinks he's a newsman. *Please.* It takes more than a sexy physique to tell a story on air.

Lucky for me, he's bending over a co-worker's computer, giving me the full, amazing view of his tight ass. I have two weaknesses in life: a muscular backside so toned you could bounce a quarter off it and Mexican food, and I'm sure not thinking about guacamole right now.

As if he can sense my eyes on him, he turns and catches me staring. My cheeks heat, and he grins that infuriatingly cocky grin with those deep dimples that actually make my panties wet. He rises to his six-foot-four height, and I pick up the pace, hoping to avoid speaking.

Get it together, Becks. Cade Hill is the last guy I would ever let ruin my plans for stardom.

"Truly Earth-shaking reporting today, Stone," he says, stepping to the open doorway.

I summon my inner goddess and put my nose in the air as I continue to the newsroom. "Stereotypical male response to a female-dominated profession, Hill."

The butterflies in my stomach do somersaults when I feel the heat of his body right behind me, but I don't slow down.

"Profession?" he says, and I hear that grin still in his voice. "What did I miss?"

"Charitable organization," I reply. "The Miss USA pageant awards more than 350 thousand dollars in scholarships every year."

"You know, we could use your hustle on the sports team," he says, and when I do stop, he extends a finger as if he'll touch my cheek. I inhale a sharp breath. "Picked up a little shine there."

He did *not* just mention my oily face... Oh, he did. "For your information, the humidity in downtown Houston was a thousand percent this afternoon."

"Funny, Pat's weather report said it was only ninety-eight

percent."

"Pat wasn't there, and neither were you." My eyes glide down his blue cotton shirt, cuffed at the elbows to show off his muscular forearms, to his Armani slacks. "It's a good thing. I'm sure you wouldn't want to ruin that ridiculously expensive suit."

"Thanks for noticing." He veers off, heading in the direction of the control room and giving me another view of that ass, but for whatever reason, he pauses and looks back. "You seem upset, Stone. Do I make you uncomfortable?"

Yes. He'd brushed against me in the break room once, and the sizzle had nearly given me a seizure. Okay, I exaggerate, but I had spilt my coffee down my skirt, all the way to my brand new knock-off Louboutin pumps.

"I'm a professional. I am not uncomfortable around anyone."

Lies, all lies! Cade Hill is the sexiest, most intimidating man I know, with a beard I might have imagined between my thighs more than once. *Shake it off.*

He chuckles and continues walking. I step over to my computer, quickly scan my inbox, and decide everything can wait until tomorrow. The six o'clock news is done, and I'm ready to get home, whip off my bra, and kick back. I'm passing our news director's office when I hear Marv call me from inside his glass-walled box. "Rebecca! Can you step inside for just a moment?"

Marv is old school, and I give my disheveled appearance a quick survey. Shirt out, shoes off, makeup melted—I've had better days. Still, I've been at KHOT five years. These guys know me.

Dropping my shoes, I step into them as I stuff the front of my blouse into my skirt. "Just heading home..." I pause when I see Cade sitting inside the door, his back to the wall. He seems confused, but I put on a smile as I focus on Marv. "How'd we do in the lineup?"

"CBS led with the plant explosion in Texas City. NBC stayed with us and covered the cellular strike blocking up traffic on the north side," he replies, glancing at three big-screen televisions mounted on the wall—all tuned to our competing local affiliates.

"Thank God we didn't get stuck in that." I drop into a chair opposite Cade.

"It was a tight turnaround, but I appreciate your hustle." He takes a pencil off his desk and rolls it in his fingers. "Watched your bit. It was decent."

Decent? I'd rocked the hell out of a silly human-interest story, but Marv can be hard to please. I take his criticism with a nod. Working for the top local affiliate in the fourth-largest city in the U.S. isn't for the thin-skinned. "Viewers will love Petal."

He doesn't look as confident, and a prickle of misgiving zips down my spine. Petal might have been spot-on, but my appearance was iffy.

A noise of heels clicking outside the door captures his attention. "Vicky!" Marv shouts. "Could you step in here a minute?"

Vicky, too? Now my throat is tight.

"What's up?" Vicky steps in the door looking professional and cool in cream-colored slacks and a green shirt that perfectly compliments her red hair. "Hello, Cade." She looks around the office and adjusts her glasses. "Hey, Becks. Nice work with those little robots today."

"Future Stepford Wives," I quip, and she laughs. "Except for Petal."

A stylish lady in her forties, Vicky Grant and I hit it off my first day, and she's had my back ever since. We both share a vision of shaking up this football-and-oil-dominated city and shining a light on projects and organizations trying to make a difference… pageants possibly included.

"The consultants arrived this afternoon." Marv pulls our attention back to him. "They gave me the feedback on our six o'clock show."

My stomach sinks. Corporate sends a pair of "insultants" (as we call them in the newsroom) twice a year to watch our broadcasts and give "constructive feedback," which essentially consists of ripping the reporters to shreds from the way we dress to how we walk to the word choice in our tags. It's brutal, and I do not want Cade in here listening to whatever they said about me.

Marv leans forward on his desk, resting on his forearms. Gray eyes lift under his bushy eyebrows. Our gazes meet.

"Okay?" I shift in my chair.

"What other projects do you have in the works, Becks?" He's back to playing with that pencil, rolling it back and forth in his fingers. "Any outside gigs in the hopper?"

"Outside gigs?" I'm confused. I spend every waking minute at this station, including weekends if there's breaking news. "I don't have time for a cat, Marv."

"Hmmm. Any interest in joining the production staff?" He glances at Vicky, and I do the same.

I can tell she's caught off-guard, but she covers it. "Er…of course, we could use someone like Becks in production. She's smarter and has more experience than any of our reporters, but —"

"Great! That's great!" Relief breaks over our boss's face, and he leans back in his chair as if a decision has been made. "Don't you think, Cade? You're in management now."

My eyes cut to him.

"In sports," he says. "I don't have any say over the regular reporters."

"Still," Marv continues. "You know what the board wants. You have eyes."

Dread pools in my gut. "Wait…" I can't hide the panic in my voice as I quickly glance from Cade to Marv. "Did you just take me off reporting? You know I've been working toward that weekend anchor chair."

Cade's brow lowers, and Marv's moment of cheer flits away. "The consultants think you might do better *behind* the camera, rather than in front of it. But don't worry, it's not the end—"

"What the fu-*hell*?" I curb the profanity. He's still my boss, but I'm on my feet. "Why would they say something like that? They loved my piece on the dinosaur excavation last summer!"

Marv's Adam's apple bobs as he swallows. It's his tell that he's nervous—which makes *me* nauseous. "They think we need fresher faces. Someone who'll appeal to the… eighteen to twenty-five age bracket."

"You have *got* to be kidding me! Those aren't the people who watch the news." I pace around the room, propriety gone.

Cade clears his throat. "Marv, I'm not sure I should be—"

"They're thinking of the advertisers," Marv continues. "Viewers don't want to be scolded by their mothers on the nightly news."

My brain literally short-circuits, and I can't decide if I'm more offended by his use of the word *scolded* or his use of the word *mothers*. "I'm single! I'm not even dating anyone!"

"Well…perhaps you should."

My jaw drops. He did not just go there. "That's sexist! My personal life has nothing to do with this job."

"This is news to me, Marv," Vicky says, her voice infused with calm. "Maybe we should discuss this in private before we make a decision."

He shrugs, eyes fixed above my head. The ass can't even meet my gaze. "Maybe there are some steps you could take to improve your on-camera look. Something around the forehead to look less...angry."

"Botox?" I snap. "Are you saying I need Botox?"

"Now, don't put words in my mouth." He rises from his chair, holding out a conciliatory hand. "I didn't say anything about possible plastic surgery. Did I, Cade?"

"Plastic surgery!" My heart beats faster and my chest rises. I twist the handles on my bag. Shit, I might hyperventilate. "I just turned twenty-eight!"

Cade shifts in his chair, and Marv continues. "Now, Rebecca, even you have to admit you haven't been yourself lately." His eyes drift to my straining waistline.

I stiffen, standing straighter and trying to suck in subtly.

"You've been with us five years without a break." He scratches his nearly white goatee. "Maybe a little R&R...combined with some good, brisk walks around the park."

"Are you calling me fat?" My question is just short of a shriek.

Marv looks like he swallowed a goldfish and isn't sure how it's going to come out.

Again Vicky attempts to calm the situation. "It's been a long day. Why don't we all get some rest?" She takes my upper arm and leads me to the door. "Marv and I will get with Liz over the next few days, and we can talk more about it then."

"Good idea," Cade says.

I allow Vicky to lead me to the door, but I'm vibrating with anger and outrage.

"Just breathe," she says a notch above a whisper once we're

in the hall.

"Oh, sure, quote classic country to me." I don't smile. It's easy for her to say. She can age all she wants in the control booth, but I have to remain eternally twenty-one.

Cade exits Marv's office and does a sudden U-turn when he sees us. I can't stop a tiny growl. "*He* should not have been in that meeting."

"I agree." Vicky's eyes narrow behind her glasses. "I don't know what Marv is thinking."

I'm still feeling sick. Production is where you work if you love TV news, but the camera doesn't love you. "Is he right, Vicky? Do I look like somebody's overweight, angry mother?"

"Of course not." She pats my arm. "I've got you covered here. Still…you could help me help you."

I halt and meet her gaze head-on. "What are you saying?"

"Stop frowning." Her eyes travel down and up my body. "Just make some changes on your end. You know…little things."

I grip her forearm. "Be brutal and pretend we aren't friends. Tell me what to do to stay in front of the camera."

Releasing a deep sigh, she crosses her arms. "Okay…but I'm only saying this because I care. You need to drop at least five pounds—at least. High-def shows *everything*."

Looking down, I see the seams straining on the sides of my skirt, and I tighten my lips. It's true. I've let things go a little bit. When my best friend Nancy had lived with me, she'd always been able to whip up my favorite Tex-Mex recipes with half the fat and calories. It had been her specialty—favorite foods with a healthy twist. Now she's at the Culinary Institute in New York chasing her dream of being on the Food Network, and I'm left with Doritos Locos Tacos from Taco Bell…and an additional fifteen pounds.

Of course, there's also the other thing.

"I guess I've been in a funk since James and I broke up…" I hope for a little sympathy. "It's hard to care what you look like naked when the chances of anyone seeing you naked are less than zero."

"You can increase those chances if you pay attention to your makeup."

I throw up my hands. "We busted our asses to file that pageant story on time. It was hot as hell in the expo center, and when I realized I'd left my blotting papers in the van, it was too late…"

Her expression changes, and my voice trails off. I know what she's going to say before she even begins.

"This is a competitive, appearance-driven field, Becks." She gives my arm a squeeze. "You can't slack off, even for a month, and expect to move up in the ranks. I'll buy you a few weeks, but you have got to show that you're making changes."

"I know." I rub my forehead. "You're right. I know you're right!"

"Get started tomorrow." She leaves me at the door and heads back to the control room to prep for the ten o'clock broadcast.

I throw my blazer over my arm and start for the door. A unisex restroom is just at the back exit, and I decide to make a pit stop before heading to my car and getting stuck in late-evening Houston traffic needing to pee.

Flinging the door open, my eyes land on the glorious back-side of none other than Captain Sexy himself. He steps away from the toilet, and not only do I get an eyeful of that sexy tush in all its toned and lined greatness, he turns before his slacks are completely over his hips, and I'm treated to a view of his long, thick… member. *If that's at ease, what must it look like at attention?*

My jaw goes slack, and the horrible meeting is forgotten as my purse plops to the floor. Never in my life have I ever wanted to increase my chances of being seen naked again. Forget being seen—I simply want to be naked all over *that…*

It. Is. Amazing.

Get your copy of THE LAST GUY today!
Available in Kindle Unlimited, print, and audiobook formats!

Read More...

By Ilsa Madden-Mills

I Dare You, 2018
Spider, 2017
The Last Guy, 2017*
(*co-written with Tia Louise)
Fake Fiancée, 2017
Filthy English, 2016
Dirty English, 2015

Very Bad Things (Briarwood Academy #1)
Very Wicked Beginnings (Briarwood Academy #1.5)
Very Wicked Things (Briarwood Academy #2)
Very Twisted Things (Briarwood Academy #3)

—

By Tia Louise
KINDLE UNLIMITED BOOKS
STAND-ALONE ROMANCES
When We Touch, 2017
When We Kiss, **coming summer 2018**
Mine, **coming fall 2018**
The Last Guy, 2017*
(*co-written with Ilsa Madden-Mills)

PARANORMAL ROMANCES
One Immortal, 2015

One Insatiable, 2015

BOOKS ON ALL RETAILERS
THE BRIGHT LIGHTS SERIES
Under the Lights (#1), 2018
"Sundown" (#2), 2018
Under the Stars (#3), 2018
Hit Girl (#4), 2018

THE DIRTY PLAYERS SERIES
The Prince & The Player (#1), 2016
A Player for a Princess (#2), 2016
Dirty Dealers (#3), 2017
Dirty Thief (#4), 2017

THE ONE TO HOLD SERIES
One to Hold (#1 - Derek & Melissa)
One to Keep (#2 - Patrick & Elaine)
One to Protect (#3 - Derek & Melissa)
One to Love (#4 - Kenny & Slayde)
One to Leave (#5 - Stuart & Mariska)
One to Save (#6 - Derek & Melissa)
One to Chase (#7 - Marcus & Amy)
One to Take (#8 - Stuart & Mariska)

Acknowledgments

Special thanks to our amazing beta readers Lisa Paul, Becky Barney, Sarah Sentz, Ilona Townsel, Lulu Dumonceaux, Tina Morgan, Tami Hall, Sheryl Parent, and Helene Cuji—you ladies are rock stars! Thank you for running your eagle eyes over our story and falling in love with the characters.

Thanks to Wander Aguiar for the gorgeous photography and to Shannon for the perfect design—inside and out!

Thanks to all the amazing authors who made time to give us a read and a little praise. We appreciate you more than we could ever say!

Thanks to all the bloggers for sharing your love of our books. You ladies are the stars of our reading world.

Thanks to Candi Kane, Give Me Books, and Social Butterfly for the fantastic promotional work!

Thank you to Caitlin Nelson and Julie Deaton for the great line and copyediting.

Huge thanks to Tia's Mermaids and Ilsa's Unicorns for the nonstop love and excitement, especially when we're in the cave bringing these characters to life. You're the reason we do it!

Thanks to Lulu Dumonceaux, Ilona Townsel, Tina Morgan, Tammi Hart, Helene Cuji, Sheryl Parent, Lisa Kuhne, and Elle King for helping Tia stay sane!

Thank you to Miranda Arnold, Suzette Salinas, Tina Morgan, Heather Wish, Pam Huff, Erin Fisher, and Stacy Nickelson for keeping Ilsa focused.

Most of all, saving the absolute best for last, THANKS to our families for the love and support, the patience and the encouragement. Mr. TL, Kat, and Laura; Mr. Mills, Eli, and Mia. We love you so much.

Stay sexy,
Ilsa & Tia

About the Authors

Wall Street Journal bestselling author Ilsa Madden-Mills and *USA Today* bestselling author Tia Louise kicked off their co-writing adventure in 2017 with the #4 Amazon bestseller **THE LAST GUY**. (They had so much fun writing that zany rom-com hit, they decided to do it again.)

Great friends, former English teachers, and southern gals in real life, they've teamed up to bring you laugh-out-loud naughty romances with strong leading ladies and sexy alpha males who know how to please their women—and who sometimes you just want to slap.

Keep up with them online:
www.IlsaMaddenMills.com
www.AuthorTiaLouise.com

Made in the USA
Middletown, DE
09 September 2022